inside the easter egg
Marian Engel

 Anansi Toronto

Cover design: Linda Bucholtz
Photo: Graeme Gibson

Published and produced in Canada with the assistance of the
Canada Council and the Ontario Arts Council by

The House of Anansi Press Limited
35 Britain Street
Toronto, Canada M5A 1R7

ISBN: 0-88784-436-7   AF 35

Canadian Shared Cataloguing in Publication Data

Engel, Marian, 1933—
    Inside the Easter egg.

(Anansi fiction series ; AF 35)
ISBN 0-88784-436-7

I. Title.

PS8559.N44I5   813'.5'4
PR9199.3.E

Some of these stories have appeared in *Chatelaine, Fiddlehead, The
Ontario Review, Fourteen Stories High* and on the CBC programme *Anthology.*

The author wishes to thank the Canada Council and the Ontario
Arts Council for their assistance.

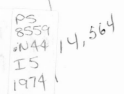

CONTENTS

I. THE MARRIED LIFE

II. ZIGGY AND COMPANY

III. CHILDREN AND ANCESTORS

for
Mary Anne Roberts

THE MARRIED LIFE

INSIDE THE EASTER EGG

WHEN Mary Abbott went to the hospital to be sterilized, she told the children she was having her appendix out. Her mother came down from Hearst to look after the children, and her husband, Osborne, went to the hospital with her to sign the permission form. "I don't think," said Mary Abbott, "that that's exactly necessary." The admissions clerk looked up without expression. "Anything that affects your marriage," she said, "must be done by mutual consent."

So Mary signed, and Osborne signed, and Osborne hung miserably around the waiting room while Mary disappeared hither and thither with candy-striped high-school girls for x-rays and tests. When he got her settled in her room, he hovered by the window, not knowing whether to go or stay. "I think," she said, "that you'd better go home and help Mother. Sundays are always so long and I don't want Henry and Georgie to start fighting."

Osborne was very tall, and very frail. He had a large head with a bulging white forehead. More than anything else, he hated noise. He was a philosopher. "And try to be patient with Mother," Mary said.

The floors in the hospital were quiet floors: there was thick cork under the tile. Mary lay back in bed, enjoying the quiet, wondering how her mother was managing. She was too old for them, she thought; well-preserved, but so bent from the harsh northern winds she was used to. She had insisted on coming. Mrs Kenney would have been better. By Wednesday she'll be ready to give up her foolish pride and let Mrs Kenney come and help. Ah well, no use worrying. Mary had a stack of magazines and books she had been saving since Christmas against her week in the hospital. She began to read.

In the morning, Mary was wheeled to the operating room on a stainless-steel cart by a cheerful little man as old as her mother. "All right, dear?" "Sure," said Mary, groggy with tranquillizer. "Are you sure you want this done?" the doctor asked — green-capped now. "It's not too late to back out." "Very sure," said Mary.

Mrs. Beatty was trying to get Henry to go to school. She offered him comfort, candy, compromise, threats. He said he would go if she would walk with him. She was seventy-eight, but she buckled her heavy coat on, and pulled up her galoshes firmly, and took Henry out on the ice. Henry wiped his nose on the sleeve of his snowsuit. She looked at his pale, tear-stained face and thought, these children need more air, more cod-liver oil. "Why don't you like school, Henry?"

"They're not nice to me, they beat me up; the principal has an iron finger and he sticks it in your belly-button if you're late." Halfway down the block he spotted a chum and the pale look went off him; he went lickety-split away from his Gran and towards school, leaving Mrs. Beatty stranded on an ice-floe, useless and annoyed.

Georgie was picked up by the nursery-school pool, and Emma went to the school for the deaf on a special bus.

At noon, Mary opened her eyes and saw Osborne's big head far in the distance, at the foot of her bed. "Hi."

"How are you?"

He was staring at her tragically, as if he had done something awful to her.

"Fine, I think. What does the nurse say?"

"She says you're fine."

"That's good."

She fell asleep again, and when she woke up he was gone.

Mrs. Beatty had tried hard to like Osborne, and had failed. Of her four sons-in-law, he was the coldest, the least cheerful. She

4

did not know how Mary stood him. They were well enough off, and him with a good job at the university, but this big house wasn't cheerful, there wasn't a bit of liveliness in it. Her own husband had been a mining engineer, they had lived all their married years up north in the bush. She didn't — couldn't — care for Toronto and its sloppy rainy snow that turned to slush every other day and then refroze, and the grey stone buildings, and waiting for buses.

Mary woke up groggily in the middle of the afternoon. She had an intravenous tube in her hand, and it hurt. A nurse, quiet as if she were on rollers instead of medical oxfords, came in, took her pulse and temperature, and removed the tube. Mary tried to sit up. There was a woman in the next bed to her now, giving instructions to one of her children on the phone. "Don't forget to put the washing in the drier," she was saying. I've never shown Emma how to work the washer and drier, Mary thought, remembering home and herself and her sisters putting steaming sheets through the wringer and the time Jeannie got her hair caught and they couldn't remember how to turn it off. I hope Mother's all right on the cellar stairs. I'd better get Mrs. Kenney in to help. She shouldn't have told Jeannie she was going to the hospital, she thought. But what else was there to tell Jeannie, the only one of her sisters she kept up with? And now that her father was dead her mother spent her life rushing from one bout of gynaecological baby-sitting to the next. She would have been hurt if Mary had turned her offer of service down, though they were not close, because Mary had been sent to boarding school in the south at fourteen, and then to university, and never come home to live again. She hated the cold.

"Hi," said her room-mate, "what did you have done?"

"Tubal ligation," groaned Mary, to be polite about it.

"Tied off, eh? No more diapers . . . wheee."

"Three kids are enough."

"You bet, I've got seven myself, and that's enough."

"What're you in for?"

"D & C. In and out, here today and gone to-morrow. General clean-up. Wanta movie magazine?" She picked up the telephone again, and Mary fell asleep.

Mrs. Beatty rammed the dishwasher back against the wall and began to teach Emma to wash the dishes by hand. Emma liked that, and she liked the way her Gran talked to her as if she wasn't deaf at all. Though it was funny the way she walked around talking to nobody all day, like to-day when Emma had pretended to have ear-ache, and stayed home just to lip-read. Gran didn't like Daddy, not at all. She went around saying he lived in his own world, and made a slave out of Mummy, who had this big house to clean all by herself, who lived like a duchess but without help, and had to wear herself out. It made Emma want to cry to think Gran didn't like her Daddy; but not very much, because it meant, too, that Gran didn't understand about philosophers, and Emma did. And why didn't Gran know that Daddy got tea in bed in the morning because he was awful at the breakfast table: it was much nicer without him because he got mad when you fought over which chair you were going to sit in.

Osborne went to the movies after visiting Mary that evening. He met Eddie and Barbara in the line-up. "I hear Mary's in the hospital. Nothing serious?"

"Appendix," said Osborne.

"Oh, come off it," said Barbara, "she told me she was being tied off. You are a liar, Osborne. Why didn't you want to tell the truth?"

"It's 'er chubes," croaked Osborne, in his best Cockney accent, which was not very good.

"You should have had it done yourself," Eddie said, "then it's not irreparable. I'm surprised at you, a rational man, Osborne."

Osborne tucked his bottom in and crossed his legs and hoped the line would move.

Mary went over the rosary of her children. She missed Emma the most, because they had special ways of communicating; or did she miss Henry the most, because he was difficult, moody, and masculine? or Georgie, because she was their Canada Council Baby, conceived during a sabbatical in England, in a house in London just off Hampstead Heath, during a time when Osborne had devilled happily all day in the British Museum and she and Emma and Henry picnicked every day on the Heath. And she was little, still, Georgie, a bumble-bee baby with fat hands.

Emma's Gran talked a lot about work, work, work; and democratic countries and people who lived like English gentlemen. Grannie Abbott never talked about work. She came up once a year from Palm Beach and there was a fuss about getting her fur coat out of storage and put back and then she was gone again. She made a fuss when Henry and Georgie wrote on the walls of her house and then said, "Hell, what'm I worried about, I'm never gonna live here again." She drank a lot of whisky.

"Why, Bill used to bring me breakfast in bed," Grannie Beatty was saying, "when the church was too far away or Sunday School was in the afternoon and we could get Neighbourly News. She's worn bone-thin, that girl, no wonder she needs an operation. If he's a professor at the sainted university you'd think he'd know better."

On Tuesday, the nurse came and took the name-tag out of the slot over Mary's bed and asked her if she'd care to speak to a sociologist who was surveying women's attitudes to this operation. Mary agreed and the sociologist came with a long list of questions on a clip-board. "Hi, Finn," she said.

But of course since he knew her he didn't want her opinions, it would spoil his objectivity. "At least let me see your questions," she pleaded.

She looked at them. "They're silly questions, did you or a woman make them up?"

The sociologist was not pleased. "The team composed them," he said.

Mary was walking now. She paced the corridors gingerly and talked to other women about their bodies. "There's not one of us with any regrets," she said firmly. "The world has enough people already, we all know that by forty we could have had twenty kids each, and how could you face that with the price of snowsuits these days? I mean, the other night in bed I was thinking, I'd like to have another little girl and call her Polly. But I thought it through and realized I liked the *name* Polly — so I could change one of the others to it without adding to a generation the best authories claim has no future. That's ridiculous."

INSIDE THE EASTER EGG

There wasn't much to talk about with Osborne. Yes, the cleaners had come. Mrs. Beatty had taken Georgie out for a walk. Yes, he had chipped the ice off the front steps. The children were fond of her — really fond (he said this with wonder in his eyes) and very happy. She was not much missed.

"Does she still tell wonderful stories?"

"That's why I'm late, I was hovering in the doorway listening."

"They start with going through the glass pane of an Easter egg, and then they're all about Up North and the mining camps, and the time we were ship-wrecked but I wasn't born yet; and the Chinese cook they had, and the time the search-party on skis had to go looking for Ron . . ."

"And the time you had to leave the house because of the forest fire . . ."

"I wish I could teach you two to get on with each other."

"She's all right, really. I just feel she disapproves of me."

"Oh, she does. She thinks you're the Idle Rich. But never mind, Osborne, I know you're not."

And they both laughed ruefully, because his mother's house cost them more than they could afford to keep in repair, that was one thing about living in something approximating the size of a castle that jealous people never took into account. "It's going to be all right," she said. Then the public address system made it all right for them. A soft Scottish voice started saying "Calling Miss Incognito, calling Miss Incognito," and they burst out laughing.

Mrs. Beatty thought the house looked nice enough when it was tidy, but that it was drab and colourless. That dark wood panelling, for instance, around the dining-room, was beautiful wood, but oh, it was dark. And the new apartment building cut off the light from the bay window. And even their pictures were all black and white. She bundled Georgie into her snowsuit, though it hurt her hands to do the little galoshes up, and took her out to the Metropolitan store, where they bought chocolate-coated raisins for both of them, and a spray of plastic rosebuds, and some plastic forget-me-nots, and some plastic fern to go with them, and at the last minute, two sprigs of plastic lily-of-the-valley, to brighten Mary's house up.

Mary was exhausted from following the D & C lady's conversations all day on the telephone, and from being a good girl about drinking her liquids, and hiking herself up on her elbows to go to the bathroom all day. She had a fever and her doctor came to see her specially. "You've been overdoing it," he said.

"I suppose so."

"There's no real problem."

"I have been said to have the constitution of a horse."

He looked at her and smiled. She thought, he makes you feel about your body as if it's a rather interesting sports car. Once she had thought doctors were special, that they knew something other people didn't, but now she was older and wiser. If even philosophers had the usual difficulties ploughing through life, doctors were not special.

"Is your husband the Abbott who was at St. Andrew's with me, Osborne Abbott?"

"Yes."

"He went on to do philosophy?"

"Yes."

"Ask him for me if he's found the Philosopher's Stone?"

"Have you turned base metal into gold?"

"No," he laughed, and flipped her nightie up, though respectfully. "That's a nice incision. You'll be able to wear a bikini. Keep the curtains pulled around your bed, and try to sleep."

Emma thought of staying home another day to listen to Gran carrying on her angry telephone conversation with God, but decided against it. It would mean she would have to go to the ear-specialist in a taxi, and she was afraid of being kidnapped.

Osborne was afraid when he heard Mary was not as well today as yesterday. He told her a jocular story about a graduate student of his who had been converted to Wittgenstein and left his wife. The nurse came in and looked at Osborne. "Why didn't you have it done yourself?" she asked.

"Listen," said Mary fiercely, "it's my body, and my business."

The next day she had a new room-mate called Rose O'Leary

9

whom the man with the operating-room cart had seen before. "Here you are again, dearie," he said. "Got your teeth out?" He checked the number on her wrist-bracelet against that of the loose-leaf folder under the pillow of the stretcher table, and Rose herself scrambled onto the table in her surgical gown without showing so much as an inch of tail. "Bye, love," she said to Mary.

"Here we go, Rosie."

"You bet, Maurie."

Mary lay in bed and flipped through the *Encounter* magazine Osborne had brought her. Her brain had melted; it did not make sense. She got up and got one of Rose's movie magazines, and sat in the armchair by the window reading it: all Kennedys and rock singers she had never heard of, not like the great days of Betty Grable and Harry James at all. A big blonde woman came in to the room in her housecoat. "You were Monday, too, weren't you?"

"Yes."

"How do you feel?"

"All right. A bit wonky."

"I feel like hell, I really do. My husband's feeling as guilty as can be, seeing me like this."

"Mine, too."

"I took Richard along to the specialist to ask about him having it done to himself, and he said, you realise Mr. Johnson there's a three percent psychological impotency rate, and he fainted dead away, the poor man."

"Oh, dear."

"Do you go out to work?"

"No, I'm home with the kids."

"I was when they were small. Are yours small? You must have started late."

"I was twenty-eight when I had Em."

"That's not so bad. I had my first at twenty-one and four afterwards, and I stayed home till the youngest was three but I got so fat: it was all that macaroni and cheese they were crazy about. I'd like to have another in a sort of a way, but my legs are bad. How are yours?"

"I had trouble with veins after the third one."

"It was a big baby, then? Well, I went on the Pill, and I had to have a bunch of veins out and I said to Richard, that's that. I love having babies, I really do, but it's hard on him, having to provide so much for them and I must say I've been a better mother since I've been out working. Happier myself, like. Don't you do anything at all outside?"

"I do some typing for my husband."

"What did you do before?"

"I was a secretary in the Iranian Oil Company. I travelled a lot; I liked that."

"Well, you can't do that now, can you? Wouldn't it be grand to just pick up and go again. Still, my gang's growing up. What does your husband do?"

"He teaches philosophy."

"What kind of philosophy?"

"Ethics."

"A man with a moral sense, then. It must be interesting."

"It is and it isn't. He needs a lot of quiet, which little kids do not provide."

"I hope you have a big house, then."

"Oh, I do."

In the big house Mrs Beatty was helping Henry make a sign, "Welcome Home," for his mother, and Emma was happily washing the knives and forks. The egg came off them better in the dishpan Gran had gone out and bought. Georgie had made a paper chain by herself before she was put to bed. "Oh Henry," Mrs. Beatty said, "you're as left-handed as your mother." Henry started to cry.

Osborne visited Mary for the last time in the hospital. It seemed a little pointless, but she was obviously lonesome, she held on to him until the announcement came, visitors must leave. "No Miss Incognito to-night," she said.

"How do you feel about coming home?"

She looked out the window where the cold world was remote in the dark. "I'm a little scared. You're so protected here. Even a week insulates you against the world. I'm afraid of going out in the wind; it's warm here."

"The kids are excited."

"I guess so."

"They're making signs."

"Oh, God bless them. It's all phoney, but it feels so good."

"Would you have wanted me to send you flowers?"

Yes, she wanted to say, yes. But she said, "They're a waste of money, they only die."

"No Miss Incognito tonight."

"We were talking to-day down the hall about having babies. It was a funny, wistful conversation. Very grisly, you wouldn't have liked it. But we didn't have much else to talk about — women from all over."

"You could have talked about Women's Lib."

"It never came up. It's maybe odd that it didn't. Is Mother looking all right?"

"She goes to bed so early, she must be tired."

"Well, you'd better go now. He says I'm fit if I don't have to pick up Georgie. I suppose Mum would think it extravagant if we got in Mrs. Kenney."

After Osborne was gone, Rose O'Leary said, "He looks like a priest."

Mary did not know whether to be pleased or not, so she said, "I don't know whether to be pleased by that or not."

"Oh well," said Rose, "it depends on which kind of priest. He's a thinker, he is."

"Oh yes, he's a thinker."

"Doesn't do him much good, does it?"

"I dunno, Rose, noise bothers him more than most, and colour, he can't stand bright colours, they distract him. But we get along all right and I like what he does. He has three books out in Amsterdam, he's well thought of."

"Well," said Rose, "Fancy me, meeting a real philosopher."

Mary thought, of all the ones I've met here, she's the only one I'll miss.

Osborne drove her home slowly, avoiding brick-paved streets where the ice had built up into ruts, though this was not necessary; it was getting in and out of the car that bothered her, having to be helped and handed like an old woman.

She was touched by Henry's sign with its backwards L; and shocked by her mother's tired look; and depressed by the grayness of the house, of the winter neighbourhood, remembering suddenly the brightness of her mother's yellow kitchen, and the urgent necessity of wherever they moved buying paint to make a yellow kitchen. The house was tidy: her mother must have slaved to get them all to put their things away. She sat down gingerly, and clutched Georgie to her knees and told Henry he could see her scar when it looked a little better, and put one arm around Emma.

Under Mrs. Beatty's regime, lunch was at twelve-fifteen. After fifty years of living on routine, she had the pulse of the world in her head. It was one that suited children admirably, Osborne and Mary less. Mary thought, I had better pull myself together and take over, but the moment she entered the kitchen her will was sapped by the lazy luxury of the past week in the hospital. She took over the management of the children from her mother, and could see her mother thinking, she's letting them get away with things. "Times have changed, haven't they, Mum?" she said.

Mrs. Beatty was the one for getting up early and hustling through the morning to save herself working in the afternoon. Mary heard her muttering as she made the upstairs beds (which Mary could not yet bend over to do) about Osborne and his tea, and the way he crumpled the morning paper sheet by sheet and left it on the floor beside the bed. "What you do, Mother, is just leave the papers there until either he or you feels like picking them up. And you pull the bed up in the afternoon, if you feel like it. It sounds disgusting, but if you can't change Osborne, you change yourself."

"But what do you do when company comes and the bedroom is untidy?"

"Good heavens, company doesn't come into the bedroom!" Then she remembered at home, ladies coming for bridge or for Church Circle, leaving the coats on the bed, doing their hair at the dressing table, and thought how well the women of her mother's generation, though they accepted a certain amount of servitude, had their men in hand. "It's just that Osborne and I have a different kind of deal," she said.

Her mother seemed so remote, a creature from another planet, with her stories of camps and decorated Easter eggs that were magic caves, and her real, acerbic bustle: always knocking things into the form that had been decreed for them: whereas Mary had no idea of what should be and simply tried to keep the rubbish of living low enough to step over.

"We're terrible about time, I know, Mum," she confessed. "But somehow we get through our lives."

"Henry gets away with murder. You mustn't let him get around you."

"Sixes are terrible liars, aren't they?"

Mrs Beatty thrashed away at the saucepans she was washing (Mary was drying) as if that wasn't what she meant at all.

Mrs. Beatty had a nap in the afternoon, and so — because she was not yet over her operation — did Mary. Georgie protested, but Mary followed her mother's habit of abandoning her sternly in her crib, because she had a green fear of taking Georgie into her bed and having her jump on her stomach. Usually, she let her go without a nap so she'd go to bed earlier at night.

Mrs. Beatty helped the children make valentines after school. She had bought doilies and red construction paper and stickers — bouquets of forget-me-nots — when she was buying plastic flowers. They sat up to their ears in Elmer's glue, and when Osborne came in he said to Mary that he wished the dining-room table had looked like that when he was a child.

Word came from the North that Ron had been laid off at the mine: suitcases flew into Mrs. Beatty's smile. Betty'd be needing her. Osborne took her to the railroad station and came back shaking his head and grinning. Emma was the one who was upset. She wanted to go on doing the dishes by hand.

"Why not, Mummy?"

"Oh, it's boring; I hate doing dishes."

"But we can talk, then."

"Darling, we can talk while we're tidying, or in the living-room." Automatically, she removed the little bunch of plastic flowers — it was real or nothing for Mary — from over the sink.

"Oh, can I have those?"

"Sure, kid. Where did she put the teapot, then?"

"In the cupboard where the whisky used to go."

"Where did the whisky go?"

"Daddy drank it, with that graduate student of his."

"Oh. Do you think Georgie'd mind if we started calling her Polly?"

"Why?"

"I was thinking in the hospital, I'd like another baby named Polly, and then I thought, I could call Georgie Polly, it's more of a girl's name."

"Georgie's a bit young, but you could call me Polly, Mum."

"Would you like to be called Polly?"

Emma shot her a rare, adoring look and clutched her bouquet to her grisly bosom.

"You got on well with Gran, didn't you?"

"Oh yes, I love Gran. She's nicer than Grannie Abbott, isn't she?"

"I don't know, because I don't know Grannie Abbott as well as I know my own mother."

"Well I think so. She tells wonderful stories. But she doesn't like Daddy much, does she?"

"She has no idea what Daddy's about and she thinks that people who get up late in the morning are bad."

"Do you?"

"Good heavens, no. Have you done your homework?"

"Yes."

"Off to bed with you now, it's half past eight."

"Gran made us all go at seven."

"So there are some advantages to having me home! Goodnight . . . Polly."

Emma darted up the dark stairwell. Mary went into the living room to join Osborne, who was reading the *Star* and crumpling the pages as he finished them. "Really, Osborne!"

"Your mother's a bad influence."

"It would be more *moral* to leave them flat so I could bundle them up for recycling."

She sat quietly, waiting for the next leaf to fall. It fell flat. She felt victorious. Then she felt very tired. "Emma's to be called

Polly from now on," she said. "And I think I'd like to wallpaper this room."

"Why, for heaven's sake? It's always been this colour."

"Well you can see why your mother got rid of it and went to Palm Beach as soon as your father died; it's so gloomy."

Osborne remembered standing lost in the blazing sun in the middle of Teheran, and a girl in a blue shirtwaist dress coming up to him, taking the guidebook gently out of his hand, and turning it to the right page for where he was, grinning at him with a smug and impish grin. "You're restless," he said, "you're losing your sense of humour. You used not to care about anything, you accepted things, everything was grist to your mill, you could live anywhere, do anything."

"Did I tell you Dr. Miller asked were you Osborne Abbott and had you found the Philosoper's Stone?"

"Kidney stone, more likely. And has he turned base metal to gold?"

She thought of her father, a big frame on snowshoes; she thought of the mines; she thought of leaving to go to boarding-school, and not looking back, of getting out of the tiny little towns and away from the cold, away from littleness and meanness and useless suffering. "I can't get over Ron's being laid off at forty-five," she said. "The mines are closing up all over, there won't be work for him."

"My paper's been accepted for the Learned Societies. I'd better go and work on it."

"I'm going to bed."

He looked at her, and she thought he looked frightened. Perhaps she still had that green hospital face that scares you. "That was fun," she said, "the night you brought me the martini in the pickle jar at the hospital."

"I'm sorry about Ron," he said, "and I'll come up and rub your back."

She looked in on the children. Henry had gone to bed in his underwear again. Georgie was flat out on her back, breathing through her mouth. She turned her over. Emma had fallen asleep reading under the covers with a flashlight. She turned out the flashlight and put it on the dresser. Was it sentimental not to take it away? "Good-night, Polly," she whispered.

She got into her own bed, thinking what a victory it would be if Osborne folded the papers instead of crumpling them up. Osborne came upstairs and advanced a philosophical proposition she was too tired to understand. "Good night, Miss Incognito," he said, switching out the light.

I SEE SOMETHING,
IT SEES ME

I see a woman with a wide, kind face, high rosy cheekbones, short salt-and-pepper hair, camel hair coat, and, at second glance, rather beautiful golden eyes. Her little boy, plainly dressed in navy blue nylon, sits quietly beside her clutching a new Matchbox toy.

The other woman with the camel hair coat and the little boy got off at Inglewood Drive. She was taller and thinner, less matronly but not younger, and wore brown vinyl boots smeared with metallic patterns: bronze, copper, gilt, silver, like the upholstery in a night club of the sort she would not go to. They were new boots, lightweight for spring. Some impulse to cheer herself, perhaps, after the long winter.

The snow has stopped. Now cold rain falls. Going up the hill the streetcar conductor stops to let a cortege come out of the cemetery. Many black cars with Chinese faces at the window cross in front of us and turn south. A woman standing by the door waiting for her stop and mine says, "Nice weather for a funeral." The conductor nods and starts again.

I see a Negro with a face like an Easter Island statue. Enormous carved cheekbones push the skin out so that it is lighter and the bones seem to shine through. He is not black, coffee-coloured rather, and the skin around the eyes is darker. It is a beautiful, solemn face.

A young Chinese boy sits in front of him, in one of the seats parallel to the road, by the door. He sits half-slouched, in a shy

18

teen-age posture, his hands hanging between his open knees. I wonder if he noticed the procession.

I tell myself, "You're getting like your mother, you always remark on race." Because the first thing she says about going to a department store is, "The clerk was a . . ." and then she narrates his history and the history of her purchase. It is part of the national heritage to go to the other end of the world and be asked by an errant fellow-Canadian, "What church do you go to?"

It is time to get off. I notice that the streetcar conductor is a nondescript one, one of the ones you won't remember. On the whole conductors are a handsome lot, seen principally in profile, their dark uniforms bringing elegant profiles out of the confusion of background. Iron-gray matinee idols with beautiful noses and keen eyes survey the intersections, sell tickets, make change, shift their gum and call out street names. A lot of them are Irish. Eamonn says the cars are dead easy to drive, though once he got lost on a sort of switching circle and went round and round at least a hundred times in the night until he figured out how to get back on the track to the carbarns. He had come on a shift from a party. It was before he went into politics.

The street is covered with a sludge of rainwater, sand, mud, and melting snow, the consistency of brown Windsor soup as served on British freighters. It is garbage day and the wind is high, there are cigarette packages and frozen food wrappers in the gutter. Sodden newspapers. The woman ahead of me has a pinkish coat with a collar that looks like a wet Persian cat.

It is three o'clock, and cold. The shopping bags are heavy. This morning I shortened my old beige raincoat. It is not warm enough, and it looks, now, in a car window, like a drooping pyjama top instead of a drooping nightgown. It will have to go, after all, and not to charity.

Shirley waves from her living room window. She is carrying Paul, who is crying. There are children in the nursery school window, but none of them are mine. The Volkswagen with the fender off is still parked in front of the house with the ruby glass hall window. The lid of our garbage can has been blown onto the Monaghans' lawn. I steel myself dutifully to clamber through the mud and get it, and then I notice something.

Something related to an article in a weekend gossip column: if you see a painters' and decorators' truck with the name on the side, ReAnning, that's a private detective. It is in front of our house. I have seen it before, though not in front of our house — from the street-car, noticing the odd name with the upper case letter in the middle. Apparently there are peepholes in the back door.

I plough through the slush to the back door with the lid and the body of the garbage can, thinking, could it be me? The idea is ludicrous: even as a child I could not keep a secret, I never make threats in my letters to MPs. No one needs to spy on me and Richard is away. Probably they're after the stewardesses across the road.

By the time I take off my boots and go to the front window the truck is gone. I think of the spy-world we live in — social security numbers identical with medicare ones, everything from your income to your liver on file. I put down the groceries and make the report:

— Subject emerged from St. Clair-Eglinton car at St. Clair subway, headed downstairs, stopped, turned, snapped fingers, went up against the trend and out the exit door. Was carrying one empty red-white-and-blue P.V.C. shopping bag, and one paper shopping bag marked "Toronto Public Libraries". Went out into the rain, shivered, ducked into the drugstore, stood seven minutes in front of magazine rack; bought one magazine, one tube of peppermint fluoride toothpaste. Fingered package of sugarless chewing-gum, put it down again.

— Subject crossed immediately with light to west side of Yonge Street, proceeded south to El Patio del Oro Arcade, stopped in front of shoe-store window. Muttered "Never mind," and entered arcade. Looked at children's clothing and entered delicatessen. Purchased half a pound of Mortadella, two knackers and two smoked sausages. Said to the clerk, "I hope they go with lentils," and, "I'm bloody tired of Anglo-Saxon food up where I live." Added to purchase one loaf of sliced rye bread, three packages of sesame snaps, two marzipan imitation fried eggs.

— Subject put packages in striped shopping bag, looked

hesitantly at Arcade Cafe, proceeded to Arcade exit and south on Yonge Street. Entered second delicatessen, fingered Easter eggs, and stared at cheese, purchased one 25¢ vial of German capers and one package king-size menthol cigarettes.

—South on Yonge street again to Rosedale Animal Clinic. Entered without hesitation and asked receptionist for cat-tranquillizers. When veterinary was called, explained that cat in question was castrated male domestic shorthair aged six, in need of rabies inoculation and nervous of cars. Veterinarian stated that it was a bad year for rabies. Subject stated that she had seen in the past year skunks, raccoons, squirrels, groundhogs, rabbits and one porcupine in her back yard, which was over the north wall of the cemetery. Vet said that tranquillizers were available at ten for a dollar. While vet wrote prescription, subject read pamphlet on animal immunization and supplied typist-receptionist with information that name of animal was "Harry". Subject paid one dollar and pocketed immunization leaflet along with plastic container of tablets. "I'll bring him for a shot later," she said.

—Subject left premises, remarking that they were smartly decorated and that business ought to be good in the neighborhood. Crossed Yonge street stealthily at Shaftesbury Avenue light (note: subject may be nervous of crossing roads), proceeded with some hesitation past the beer store through the parking lot and the bridge-overhang to the government liquor store.

—Subject walked back and forth in front of the wine racks for nine (9) minutes muttering to herself, then moved to the wine-consultant's desk and spoke in an inaudible respectful voice. Consultant shook his head.

—Subject proceeded to counter, filled in order, signed form, tore form up, chewed pencil, filled second order form. Gave order to east cashier along with crumpled ten-dollar bill. Collected change and handed order-slip to clerk. Marked receipt and stuffed it in her wallet. When clerk returned with bottles she said, "I don't want the Medoc if it's not a '64. That was the year they needed only one more rain and got it. Before Cyril Ray died." Clerk frowned, ripped tissue-paper from wine bottle. Medoc was '64.

—Subject put two bottles in each bag and walked uphill to St. Clair station; boarded the St. Clair-Eglinton streetcar and proceeded to residence without speaking to anyone.

Now the '64 Medoc is in the kitchen cupboard, the knackers and Mortadella and capers are in the fridge, the marzipan eggs are sitting in an attempt at wit on the table waiting for the children. I notice that we are out of instant coffee. I notice that the sewing machine and the vacuum cleaner need to be put away. I notice that the castrated male domestic shorthair is hungry. I notice that the house is as usual untidy. I notice, because now that the painter and decorator ReAnning is gone, who else will notice?

MINA AND CLARE

His wife was a big Dutch girl, born in the East Indies and raised in the West. She hated the winter, and stayed inside for weeks at a time mourning the sun. When February was at its lowest point, however, she would bestir her big frame, raise her slow green Modigliani eyes to the East and prepare a list of errands for him: he was to drop everything and go to the Dutch butcher, the Philippine grocer, the street markets, everywhere. Then she would have the ingredients for a rice-table, and she would shoo the children into the icy wind and spend five days grinding peanuts, marinating chickens, pounding spices and grinding coconut. The house filled with the odor of shrimp paste and a kind of rotted-fish condiment called blachan. Then she invited the horde—his high school friends, his university friends, his law-school friends, his clients, the friends she had made amongst his. He loved to see her at the feast, her eyes incandescent.

He had started independent practice at twenty-eight, beginning with his friends' house-purchases, his mother's friends' wills. Now he was thirty-eight and heavily involved in his friends' divorces.

The situation depressed them both. Mina received the wives' complaints and confessions in the afternoons. At the office he had to decide which member of the couple to act for. At night, they clung to each other, feeling innocent, sexually opaque, unable to understand their friends' declivities. "It isn't," he would say in dis-

23

gust, "as if Brian's going after anything but a piece of skirt ten years younger than Ann." She would agree with him and look fearfully at her body in the mirror. He would feel depressingly smug. "Sexual propaganda," he would say, "that's what it is, sexual propaganda."

For aside from Mina's abomination of, fear of, the winter, they were happy. They had two green-eyed beautiful children, and Mina, who was lazy, liked staying at home. She had help because she expected to have help, and Bob could pay for it. She read a lot. She liked company, she took an interest in what Bob did, she was good to the children. They lived near a park.

But the broken marriages hurt her and threatened her. She began to attribute them to the long winters. "They're not that long," he said. "Come now, we're pretty far south for Canada."

"For Canada."

"In parts of Norway they don't see the sun for months."

"Why do these men have to go around with girls, young girls? Why do these women who have everything nag and complain? Why do they make their lives miserable, miserable and dull?"

Bob, who had never been anywhere duller than the Dutch West Indies, said he thought the misery came from the pursuit of women and property having been approved activities when he and his friends were boys. Now that society appeared to have moved on to higher things, his friends were left behind teething on thighs and fenders. And went on to dissect the matter of the Merritt settlement, which would involve Stan's selling the house to give Coral her equity.

"It's stupid," Mina said. "They could live together and he could keep the little green girl as a mistress. Because with a new wife he will start all over again and do the same thing, and have a heart attack and need Coral to nurse him."

"He says sex is better with the other one."

"Oh-la-la, sex. Of course it is easier to get it up with a new girl. He should be too busy."

"Coral talks all the time."

"He wants a woman with a perfect body, his wife's is marked by child-bearing, she is tired by looking after that big boring house, she knows no other entertainment than buying, buying, buying. Then she goes out and gets a job and he hates her independence. The Peters are the same: he likes to chase young girls, she hates to stay at home waiting up for him, he objects when she makes herself more independent, so they divorce, causing their children agony, to make a new arrangement that is exactly the same. As for the Parrishes . . ."

"There's no doubt in my mind that Clare is a nymphomaniac."

"Nonsense, Bob. Clare is very nice. She is the only wife of your friends who is not silly."

"They seem to be the one couple who ought to have divorced."

"That's because Bill is your oldest friend and you do not like to see him hurt. But I think Clare gives herself, really gives herself, and is good at heart. She is very beautiful and has no morals, that is all. She is also good to their children, but very vulnerable to people in distress."

He hummed "For those in peril on the sea . . .", but she did not see the joke. "It's hard on Bill," he said.

"Ach, perhaps you are right, he has tolerated her, but he will not be able to always, it hurts too much. But Clare is not sordid, and I like the way he does not possess her: she is not a piece of real estate for him. Most of your friends treat their women as if they were houses—they move out of them frequently."

"And the price keeps going up."

"I must ask Clare and Bill to dinner. It is so rare when one likes both members of a couple."

His eyes gleamed, hoping for a nasi-goreng, sati, satori. Then she said, "But I am not going to do entertaining for you this winter, Bob. I am going to take the children home."

He did not want her to go. He was afraid of being left alone in the long vulnerable winter. What would he reach out to in the night? But the decent thing to do was to send her graciously. She had had twelve winters here, she had faced the gales with courage and the life here was not her kind of life (though when they went to her parents in the Antilles he could catch no glimpse of Conrad, of papaya beaches, of southern lushness except in an unpleasant kind of derelict laziness among the servants), she had every right . . .

"It is time the children knew their grandparents better," she said, "And you can see more of your mother."

So for an entire school year he was to be alone. His mother suggested he move in with her; his friends waited for a pair of female jaws to snap.

Bill and Clare came to him, not, he was surprised to learn, for a divorce (to his sorrow, because, given Clare's income from her good government job, and their property, and Bill's devotion to the children, it would have been an interesting case), but for a change in testamentary guardianship arrangements, Bill's mother having died. They visited after he had done ten minutes' business. "You're batching it, aren't you? Everything all right?"

"Mina couldn't bear another winter here."

"I've never seen anyone hibernate the way she does. She *suffers.*"

"I hated the thought of her going, but. . ."

"Oh, Bob, she's been faithful to the point of being noble, she's the epitome of a good wife. . ."

Bob stared at Bill, who seemed as long and dreamy as ever, but shabbier. They had known each other since childhood, but he wondered how much he knew of how Bill worked—except of course at the university—how he withstood Clare's. . .charity.

And she sat there with her beautiful clear nun's face, long legs crossed under a little kilt, showing stockinged thighs. He thought of Reg Hammond's saying tights were hell to get off and felt a fool for never having tried.

"Lunch?" he asked.

"I've a lecture," Bill said.

"I'm free," said Clare. And with a ghastly lurch he fell in love with her.

At lunch she talked about how good Mina was, and how unusual. "Yes," he heard himself saying, "Yes, but. . ."

"But what, Bob?"

"But . . ." and what was it that had nearly crept out? He did not know. The finger of a fossil of a dream. "But she's not here."

Clare laughed.

26

He did not want to love her. He told himself that his body wanted to bed her, but he did not love her; it was not right to love outside your family. He went to see his mother.

"Oh," she said, "isn't it wonderful, you turning up like this. I've asked Clare and Bill for dinner. I've hardly seen them since Hazel died, and I do so like to keep in touch. Jean will set another place at the table. Take off your jacket. You look all in. There's cranberry cocktail. How are Mina and the children? Does she write every week like the good girl she is?"

Bob, settling into a household Mina could never bear to be in, felt disloyal. Though Mina had been right to refuse to have her life managed by his managing mother, who should have had a business to run.

Yet, as his mother said, it was like old times, Bob and Bill and Clare—and whatever had happened to Mary Lou, Bob's old flame, such a lovely girl. Jean handing round overdone roast beef that Mina couldn't stand on Indian Tree plates, Mother as usual trumpeting on about weddings, funerals, the state of the nation, the Queen, the Flag, the book about the railways. She and Clare had always got on well, as Bob and Clare had. Bob wondered on what dim day long ago he had failed to make the Clareward decision.

"My goodness," his mother said over coffee and after-dinner mints, "my goodness, you must miss Mina, Bob."

"I do."

"Of course it gives you so much time to get on with your other projects."

"What other projects?"

"Well, there's always so much to do, isn't there? But it's too bad you haven't finished your book."

Once, as an excuse for absenting himself, he had muttered something about writing a book.

"What's this? What's this?" asked Bill and Clare. Sitting across the room from him on the chintz sofa that had once been brown fuzz that hurt your bare legs. Clare's bare-looking legs beside Bill's long crushed tweed trousers, comfortable.

"Oh, one of those things that never came off."

"Poor Bob," his mother said. "He's like his father, so cautious he doesn't get around too much." Flashing her rings.

Clare came, casually, to the house the next evening. To borrow a book. He was trying to work on a case, absent-mindedly, was glad to see her, felt twinges of conscience. Thou shalt not covet. Thy neighbor's wife. So this is. . .

Her body was not at all marked by childbearing. And it was not difficult to betray his best friend.

But he was not capable of being dishonest about emotions. For the next week he was enveloped in guilt, overthrown by a sick-hearted longing for her: her animation, her loping ease in the world, her lovely intelligent, heart-shaped face, her straightforwardness in bed. He felt free with her.

One night he told her that he hated to lose Bill. "You don't have to," she said. "Just keep sober and run a compartment through your head. That's all there is to it. Bill and I have a pact, we do what we want, but we never confess. You please me, I've always been fond of you. Don't have the grumpies because you're ashamed. Mina's away. You have to go to bed with someone. Why not me?"

He had said to Mina that she had the morals of a mouse.

He had meant to go to Aruba for Christmas, but the court schedule and some real estate work kept him home. He had a romping time with Bill and Clare, saw as much as he could bear of his mother, visited an uncle in a nursing home: the time went by.

He grew to dread the return of the sun. He loved as he had never thought of loving getting up early to smash at the ice on his sidewalk; he complained when it became easy and punky and failed to tax his arms. The sun was his enemy: when it returned he would have to give up Clare. No, he would not think of leaving Mina for her, but now, at this mad winter season, it was the time to be with one of his own.

He separated himself from thinking of Mina. Though he knew it would hurt her, he dictated letters to her to his secretary. While she was out of sight the figure in the landscape was Clare.

But the spring was advancing dangerously. Bill and Clare asked him to the ceremonial tapping of the maple trees on their lot. Half of his Toronto was there, with wives and kids. He sulked and hated it.

He grew restless, possessive of Clare. He disliked this in himself, but knew possession to be part of his personal law. He began to brood about whether she was still sleeping with Bill, about whether he was one of many—though government employment rules seemed not quite lax enough for that, and Bill wasn't willing to babysit every evening.

And Clare began to be restless, late for appointments.

His office life went on as before. Everyone was dutiful and efficient, even he. But there was a tear in the fabric of his life, and sometimes he felt it.

One afternoon the air was soft. He stayed late at the office because Clare was meeting him at six. His secretary left with a glance that made him turn guiltily to the case he was studying. He dismissed the juniors. It was nearly six when the doorbell rang, and something happened inside him that could have been heart leaping or cannon exploding or a signal from Portnoy, and caused him to run to the door.

It was not Clare, but an odd, rough fellow he had seen somewhere before—yes, the young fellow who helped Mina in the garden. Whom she liked, who amused her: rough-and-ready, but quite unspoiled, as she said, by the worst things about civilisation. Very stupid, but very real.

"Mr. Baker, can I have a word with you?"

"Certainly, come in."

Rough, yes. Hands big as hams—big Dutch hands, he thought, though he was no Dutchman, and no servant. The look about him you saw in court: cocky: you can't catch me, I'm the gingerbread man. The look of a tricky four-year-old.

"What's your trouble, Andy?"

He flaked his body into the client's chair, flicked ash on the rug, ground the shortest butt in the world into the big ceramic client's ashtray, sighed, burped, stuck his big thumbs in frayed and invisible vest pockets. "Well, I figure the wife's torn it this time. I didn't mind about the nigger. . ."

"Negro," Bob corrected automatically.

"Nigger, while I was in the Don, but them Lexies. . ."

It took a long time to sort the story from the gesticulations. The big steel-toed boots worked their way to his desk. "I figure, now, you're a lawyer, a real lawyer, you know what to do, like. She's got one of them legal-aid guys working for her, but I don't like to take nothing from nobody, specially the government. I figure, if you're a man, you pay."

"Maybe that's so."

"Anyway, them legal-aid guys, I had them before; either they're young fellers with long hair and the magistrates don't like them, or they're punks who can't get any business on their own. So I said to myself, I said, said I, I know a good lawyer, a real big lawyer, so I'll git him. My money's as good as anyone else's, isn't it?"

"Sure, Andy."

"What I meant about not taking from the government is this, see: I mean when they lock me up, they're obliged to feed me, like, legally and morally obliged. But I don't want no legal-aid lawyer this time, not this time. Yer wife's been good to me, giving me work around the house and passing down the snowsuits for the kids, and I figure, this time, I'll pay them back: I'll give him a real good case to work on."

"So what's the problem?"

It was not, in the end, one he wanted to be paid to solve. It had its ramifications in a life-style that made him feel middle class and experientially retarded. It seemed that the House of Correction for Women was full of Lexies, and while Andy had had his moments—but she had, too; she was only a little bit of a thing, she had four kids in four years and she didn't gain an ounce, her waist was no more'n this big around, she could get attention, all right, and she did, she'd do anything with anybody. But since he hadn't screwed around with any of the guys in the Don—oh, there were a lot of them there, all right, they'd be up your ass in a minute if you didn't keep your fingers in it—he didn't see why she had to go with the girls, like. And was that grounds?

Bob questioned him further, and in the course of the conversation counted fourteen good occasions for divorce. He had seen many judges' eyelids fall in a knowing way when they were confronted by this kind of story. And here was one of its authors handing him an ill-got fistful of earnings.

"What does she have to say about you?"

He listened. The story was again so incredibly outside his experience that he had no way of judging it. It belonged to another world, it had nothing to do with the middle-class morality that he and Mina had defended from winter after winter. It was a world of do-what-you-want and damn the consequences that came through to him. It made his friends' cavortings look half-hearted. Here was a man who had touched what reformers called the fabric of life and left a big fingerprint on it. Sexually vastly more experienced than Bob himself was, maritally unprotected (to call Clare promiscuous beside this story was ridiculous)—an alcoholic from the age of sixteen, full of tales of rape and guns and garotting, chain-whipping, child-molesting: a big comic-book story kid, gruesomely aware that the system could be made to work by playing on genteel feelings. Bred by violence on ignorance, but somehow innocent and playful.

"What is it you really want?" he asked.

The mouth fell agape. The kid was twenty-four and all his molars were gone. "I dunno," he said.

"Can you look after four kids by yourself?"

"Two," he said, "the little feller died, and Andrea, she's retarded so bad she's up near Peterborough. The other two are okay. Maybe if I could find me a good woman. . ."

"If you get your divorce and custody, Legal Aid would leave you your savings for food and clothing for the children. I'll take your case very cheaply, but I won't take it for nothing, because Legal Aid exists, and exists for people with problems like yours."

"I won't take nothing for nothing."

"You may be able to get custody if you can prove she's as bad as you say."

"Oh, that I can do, all-righty."

"With your record you may have to consider making them wards of the Children's Aid."

"Them social workers, some of them's all right and the rest don't know—how can I put it polite?—which end is up."

"We're all pretty narrow once we're educated, Andy. We get pulled out of your world into something more protected."

"That's what I mean, you don't know which end is up."

"I'm sure you're right. I couldn't manage the way you have."

"You got a good wife, that's what counts."

"Call me Monday. By that time I'll have seen what kind of help you can get at the family court."

"You'll take me on, then?"

"More likely I'll pass you on to the best possible hands. Would that suit you?"

He shifted uncomfortably, looking in Bob's face to see if this was something that would hurt. "I went around and couldn't find your wife," he said.

"She's home visiting her mother."

"Gee whiz I'd like to go away somewhere like that."

"So would I."

"Okay, thanks a million. I'll call you Monday. . .sir." The handshake was bone crushing.

It was seven. He wondered if Clare was waiting outside. No. He phoned her number. Bill answered. "No, Bob," he said, "No. Not you, Bob. She's beautiful, she's witty, she's a good lay, we all love her; but not you, Bob."

He went home. He was sick in the toilet. He went to bed and stayed in bed. On the Sunday he called his mother. She sent Jean with books and soup. He phoned Clare, and Bill answered. "What have you done with her?" he asked.

"I spanked her and sent her to bed without her supper."

On the Monday he hobbled into his office and fixed up a family court connection for Andrew Best, not feeling himself qualified to sort out such a superbly complicated life. Then he went down to his travel agent's and found he could get onto a plane to Aruba that left from Montreal in the afternoon. Which he did.

He envisaged her lying naked on the beach with a paramour. In fact she was lying lonely on a bedspread stencilled with tulips. In her father's stark Dutch house, weeping. She buried herself in him. They made love.

Then she wanted to catch up on the news. He told her about the weather, about his mother, about Andrew Best. "Oh," she said, "they play every game they see on the television, in the movies. They always get caught, those two. Dreadful things happen to them. One day he is digging in my garden, the next he gets drunk and thinks it will be fun to rob a bank. Underneath, he has some kind of intelligence. How are Bill and Clare?"

He parted the curtains and stared into the brief dusk of the shining town. Now, it looked wonderful. But he had spent a winter here before, he knew there was no elbow-room on islands. Though now that he had the sun, the prospect of curious gables, he did not know what to think about Bill and Clare, except that Bill was right, he had been playing the wrong game for himself. Then he noticed he no longer thought Clare was wicked, and he smiled from the sunlight: "Oh, they're all right: the same; you know."

Mina stretched. "Tonight, we go out and eat, really eat. There is a new man from Sumatra who makes something so good you wouldn't imagine it. Sates and sambals. Ach, you can get all the things here, the climate is right. We shall eat. I have waited a long time for you." Then, "On the plane on the way down there was that movie *Claire's Knee,* and I got jealous and all winter I have mourned for you."

Then the children came racing in with their grandfather, and threw off their European manners and enveloped them.

THE SALT MINES

SHE was guilty, of course, but it did not really bother her. For one thing, the quality of guilt was the same as ever; it was the same twinge she felt when she was out on her own and she thought she might have left the gas on and blown the house up, or earlier, when she was seven or eight, and the colors the church was painted, relentless brown and yellow, reminded her of excrement, and she was guilty.

Somehow she had expected this guilt would be different, but it was not. It was no worse, she discovered, to be guilty for real sins than to pull along the same inborn, inbred, leaden load of shame she had known all her life. I might, she thought, have been sinning all the time for all the difference it makes.

Yes, she still thought it was a sin. It was delicious, but she had been trained to think of it as a sin, the law said it was a sin, the Commandments said it was a sin: it was sin. If Barney or her mother ever found out, or worse still, his mother . . . the fat would be in the fire.

And yet, and yet . . . she was driving over flat spring fields towards Uli. The sky was blue, convex with light and warmth. It seemed to be preparing itself to receive meadowlarks. Fat groundhogs surveyed the world from fenceposts. If this is sin, I love it, she thought.

It was so long since she had been in love this way. Even, perhaps, twenty years. The soaring of the spirit, the impatience, the

34

singlemindedness: she recognized them; thought she had buried them long ago; felt, herself, resurrected. "My heart is like a singing bird . . ." and all that, she quoted.

I could lose everything, she thought. Home, children, property (half of it, maybe more, Barney was a lawyer, sharp,) reputation certainly. I don't care. The world well lost. Another cliché. At least I am not dead. It's years since I cared whether I was alive or dead. Good for Uli. Cheers for Uli. Large, obscene kisses for Uli. Who has brought me out of matronly virtue — here.

Yet she worried about Barney. She didn't worry about the kids, who were so self-absorbed and convinced she was senile that she wouldn't rock them. Even if they found out, they wouldn't believe it. They thought she was eighty, but Barney . . . who knows how he would react, she thought?

Such a nice man, a good man, Barney. Why she had married him. Thoroughly decent. But deep inside him, where it had taken her several years to ferret it out, was a core of righteousness, a firm concept of how the world should operate, and what her place was in it. This core was formed in 1895, the year his mother was born. Barney, she thought, will be deeply shocked.

This thrilled her. Yes, she wanted, meanly and indecently (she had talked about this to Uli who thought that whatever Barney's shortcomings were, she should be kinder) to shock him. Shake him up. Dance naked before him. Look. It's me. Shaking her breasts in front of him, waggling her hips. Look, Barney. This is what you married. A living, breathing, human woman. Me.

What would he do?

She lied to herself. She had fallen in love before. When Grace was three. With a doctor who lived down the beach, a fair Englishman who took early morning walks and stopped often to talk to her. Barney asked her what was upsetting her. She told him, foolishly. He gave her a blank straight stare and suggested they both regard it as an illness from which she would recover.

She stopped the car and laughed. Looked at the blue hoop of the sky, the flat fields punctuated with telephone poles. Illness. My God, she thought, what is the logic of that? You love someone better than me, therefore you are ill. If he finds out about Uli, he'll lock me in the insane asylum.

She still wanted to rub his face in it. Notice me! she was crying.

Uli didn't want to be noticed. He suffered no exhibitionist qualms. One thing he had told her: "I am the invisible man. I have lived in this town since you were five years old. No one but Van Horne has ever accepted me as an equal, and I have never had my existence recognized in any important way. You could make love to me in the middle of Main Street and tell them you were giving me remedial English lessons and you would get away with it. You are safe, Ruth. You are safe."

She started the car again. She was two lines over from Uncle Doug's farm; everyone around here was a relative and none of them had heard of remedial English lessons. Green shoots were pushing in neat, almost compulsive rows in the clayey fields. The fence-side hawthornes were in bloom. She drove to Uli.

Fifth line, sixth concession. He was working on somebody's oil rig today, one he particularly liked. Machinery first installed in the 1850's, once run by a steam engine. She could smell the oil on him when he came back from one of these places, see the engine grease, still faintly black after can after can of Snap, ingrained in his thick fingerprints and stubby nails. These little oil wells were all over the township. Long poles jerked out from the machine-houses slowly, in a rhythmic rigor mortis. Same poles originally cut, back there when the oil rush was on and Oil City, poor old rundown Oil City, was a boom town. The oil preserved them. She thought back. Mercy, when the Joyce brothers first shoveled down for water on their place, and nothing but black muck came up. . . . Having to bring water in in tanks all the way from the lake, and they paid ten dollars an acre for the land. The scandal. . . .

One of Aunt Doll's brothers had a well. Kept it going all these years. Now he was eighty and getting thirteen dollars a barrel. Or something. The tank trucks came around from the refineries and slid their probosces into the storage tank, sucked the oil into their cavernous bellies. The reverse of delivery.

Uli had made everything new for her.

He was standing by the road. She had known him since she was five, a huge man with a big, round face. It was crazy. He was her lover now. Once he had been the man who pulled trains with his teeth. A poor D.P. who didn't speak any English, too huge for any of the clothes they had to give away at the church. Who lived in a little shed he built himself in Mr. Zeidman's junk yard, better than a guard dog. At first, the librarian had not wanted to issue him a card. He had no proper address, and what would a man like that . . . Mr. Zeidman had told the chairman of the board on her.

After that, when she and her mother went to the library on Friday nights to read *Punch*, she always saw Uli there. Quietly reading. He was so big, they always expected that when he went down the front stairs they would explode. But he turned out to be a nice quiet man, refined, for a foreigner.

He saw her, waved, grinned. Climbed into his truck and waved her to follow.

Oh, she thought, I'll follow. Anywhere. You, I'll follow. You were a grown-up when I was a child; a stranger. Now, we're almost the same age.

Or am I six to his sixty and this is some Lolita number we're doing?

There were evil voices inside her sometimes.

He had a little Datsun pickup he drove on these expeditions — a small, neat truck. The back was full of machinery lashed tight and secured under old tarpaulins. He took care of things.

He zigzagged among the concession lines. Dry gravel spun on the bottom of her car as she followed him. Two o'clock. Ready when he said he would be. You didn't have to wait around for Uli. "Clockwork," he said to her, "those machines are old, but very beautiful. As simple as clockwork. When I cannot get a part, I make it. Machines are not mysterious. They are made. When you go to the antique shops, buy me nice things of brass. Like that clock your mother was throwing out and you gave me. It had many nice wheels and screws."

So do you, she thought.

She had never known she was like this. Vulgar.

It gave her great joy to be finally vulgar. Sometimes at night she felt like braying for him.

He stopped in the middle of nowhere. There was level ground by the wire fence, where they left their cars, but no gate. He took her arm. "Come on, climb over."

37

"Where are we?"

"You will see."

She went over the fence into his arms. He held her until her head stopped ticking busily. They held hands. He led her through hawthorne scrub and dying old apple trees: once an orchard. The earth was sandy. Young poison ivy springing up, the curse of these parts. A few birds making nesting noises, a cow bawling far away. Otherwise, no sound. She waited for him to speak. Suddenly, he stopped in the middle of a path that led nowhere. "Here," he said.

She looked and saw nothing. Then he moved to the left a little, bent down, and picked up a big wooden cover like a well-lid. Some kind of mine shaft, with a new ladder in it.

"What is it?"

"Don't you trust me?"

"I don't trust holes."

"Come, I will show you. It's quite safe. I have been down here before to work on the pumps. Come, Ruth. It's beautiful."

He went first. She faltered down the ladder, hating going backwards. Better when she came up.

"There, it's the last step. Put your feet down. Now, close your eyes for a moment, until you get used to the light. All right, open them."

He had a flashlight. He swung its beam around. They were in a salt mine. It was beautiful, crystalline, white. "Oh," she said, sucking her breath in, like a child.

"I wanted you to see it. There are several of them, but they are not used any more. They will be used to store oil, next year."

Then: "How long do we have, Ruth?"

"Two hours, I guess. I don't want to be late."

As usual, they were shy of each other at the beginning. Then they made love with great ceremony, lolling on hard white surfaces, rolling in the powdered salt of the floor, licking each other, laughing.

"You are the queen of it, Ruth," he said. "The queen of all the salt mines."

She wanted to say, only if you are king, but she knew she must not. He had to go on working at the plant; Barney was vice-president, she belonged to the town, she could not run away.

When it was time to leave, she, who never cried, started to weep against him. He held her in his big arms. "Ruth, Ruth."

"It's too beautiful. I don't want to go up again."

"Don't be a baby. It's easier to go up the ladder than come down. It is four o'clock. We must go now." He was firm, almost cross. Impatient, certainly. He frightened her a little. She followed him obediently.

Half way up the ladder she turned her head. She thought, I could let go, float back down in that miracle, stay forever.

He called her up harshly. Once again, she followed.

After he replaced the well-cover he took her by the shoulders and shook her. She began to sob again. She thought, I am being boring, but I must cry, and began to howl as if all the grief in the world was in her. Under the hawthorne trees, she held onto Uli for dear life. "I'm sorry," she sobbed.

"Don't be sorry. It is good to cry."

"I felt you were taking me away from paradise."

He hung his head. "That is all I can do."

"I'm all right, now. I think I can drive. It's late."

"When he goes to Montreal will you come to me?"

"Yes, but I'm running out of people to lie to the kids about."

"Don't lie. Wait until they are in their rooms. Come on foot. Come along the beach. Knock on my window. We will spend all the dark hours together."

We will spend all the dark hours together.

"Uli, some day they are going to find out."

"Some day," he said softly. "Some day. Do you want them to find out?"

"No." Then with a sharp little breath. "Yes."

He frowned. "Be patient, Ruth, be patient."

"I was standing on the library steps. You put your hand on my arm. I wanted to scream *rape*. I had known you all my life. Suddenly you were there, and it was — like this — for us."

"We are lucky. Be patient. In the future, we will be more lucky. I know, Ruth."

She hung her head. All her life she had been measured, careful. Now, a woman with half-grown children she wanted the earth to fly open for her. Perhaps it had.

THE SALT MINES

She followed him until the road before the highway, where he turned off. She drove through the industrial belt, past the plant, hoping to see him turn his truck in the lane. No. She stopped and started and stalled in the rush-hour procession. The river shone. There were no more Indians where there used to be Indians, but somehow there were still Indian dogs loping along the side of the road, brown-eyebrowed. They should have had more sense, she thought. Maybe they were following their instincts.

Barney was reading the paper. He did not notice she was late. She went into the kitchen and took lamb chops out of the freezer. She opened a can of green beans and put a lettuce in the sink. She went into the bathroom and looked in the mirror. She always thought it should show, that she should look different. She looked just the same. She closed her eyes and was back in the white crystal cave he had taken her to, going down, down, into whiteness. Lying with him. Being free with him. There's no barrier between us, no hindrance. We are one flesh. I never knew it could be like that.

Or had it been like that once with Barney, before they had land, mortgage, children, twenty years of pettiness. . . .

We don't live together, she thought. I would want to tidy away his clockwork wheels. I would change him. He's perfect now. Perfect? That strange, huge man who in winter wore an awful magenta satin windbreaker, Uli the DeePee who thumbed through the newspapers every . . .

You could look at things from the inside, from the outside, get different pictures. Fascinating. Here, she'd lived here so many years. . . .

She pulled her comb through her hair and felt and heard salt falling on the plastic tiles of the bathroom floor with the faintest tinkle.

"Hey, Mum, what're you doing in there, the lamb-chops need turning."

"Oh, I'll just be a minute. Turn them over, will you?"

Five minutes later they were polishing the whole meal off. "Good supper, Mom."

"Where are you off to?"

"Basketball practice."

"Grace?"

"Going over to Lynn's."

What are you up to, my girl? Ruth thought. You've a pussycat's grin on your face. "Come back by eleven, it's a school-night," she said. Who had herself barely lived because she was not allowed to go out at night at that age.

"Barney, are you going out?"

He was watching the television news. It took a minute for her voice to reach him. Then he half turned. "Oh. Yes. Tonight. Board of Stewards at the church, I think. Leaving you alone again. Poor Ruth."

I don't want to live with him, Ruth thought, though I'd do that rather than lose him. He doesn't want to live with me. He's never had a woman there to tidy his clockwork away. Or has he? No, we were meant to spend the dark hours in a blinding white place, where the crystals are pure and cool; and there are no mothers or fathers or children or dogs, only ourslves and this white, crystalline non-sand, and all the books we have read on Friday nights at the library, and our own, beautiful clockwork. "Oh," she said, "I might go out later for a walk on the beach, I'm restless in the spring. Or I might do the mending. Don't worry about me." Hoping there was no martyrdom in her voice.

After they left she sat in her winter coat on the steps leading down to the beach. It was cold, but the moon gleamed on the waves, and the waves sucked enthusiastically on the shore. She had no intention of going to him tonight. She was not young enough to be greedy. But she would go, would go soon. And when it was warm enough to swim, she would swim from her house to his, and arrive on his doorstep a shimmering, shivering trout.

I should be guilty, she thought. I should be guilty. But salt is really not at all like sand.

AMARYLLIS

HE was the cleanest baby they had every seen, so fastidious that his mother was worried about him. His nanny, however, assured her that he was a bright little fellow; and wasn't it a blessing to have a sweet little boy after all the big lolloping girls.

He was not sure why he was obsessed with order: it had something to do, he thought, with the hugeness of everyone around him, which amounted (because he remained undersize until he had chicken pox in his late teens and 'shot up') to gross indecency since he viewed his parents and his sisters from low and unflattering angles. What he was sure of was that for him, everything had to be tidy and intact. He knew it annoyed his family, he knew that his mother particularly considered him to be lacking in spirit, and also, from a very early age, that he was himself, complete as an egg, and would always be this way, and annoy them.

They were prosperous; they lived in one of the great solid houses on the mountain of Montreal; there was never any problem with money. When he decided to make his career in the university, where he could order facts as he ordered his life, no one protested. This was not the kind of mind that would bring scope and drive to the family business, it was a fussy mind, it might, even, for all they knew, be the mind of a homosexual. They gave him his choice of the universities. He went to McGill and Harvard and Oxford and was very happy, and obstinately although fastidiously heterosexual.

His trouble with women was, however, that he liked intellectual women, and the intellectual women he ran into were not interested in housekeeping, and he had friends with similar problems. None of them wanted to marry cows who ran splendid establishments but had nothing to say, but the good minds they met refused to deal with cupboards and scrubbing brushes or even servants. Gloomily, and perhaps too earnestly, he tested his women friends and came to the conclusion that the man who said that brainy women don't wash their hair was right.

Thus he was a bachelor of thirty-one, and well established in his field, when he accepted a vacancy in his discipline at McGill and returned to Montreal, not, firmly, to the house on the mountain, but to a modern bachelor apartment which he fitted with books and white blankets, glass and white plastic furniture, white broadloom.

His mother, having fallen into the habit of introducing young people to each other when she was marrying off the girls (she had done this with distinction), immediately arranged a set of dinner parties for him. His work load was heavy, and he would dash home looking (for him) dishevelled, and sit grumpily in the grand dining-room beside or across from the candidates she had chosen, who were on the whole ill-formed or ill-informed, for the girls of their set who had wits had gambolled away on their own years ago. Some of them, he knew, were both brainy and neat and he had missed his chance with them.

So for most of his first year at McGill he was unhappy, and he earned the reputation of being not an eligible bachelor, but a crusty one, though his social coinage remained valuable because of his surname. Towards the end of his second term, at an interdepartmental meeting, he ran into a friend of his undergraduate days, a gusty left-wing anthropologist called Ziggy Taler, an irrepressibly untidy man, but a brilliant one. He took Ziggy, who was between wives, home for a drink after the meeting.

"Christ, Alex," Ziggy said, looking around the bachelor nest, "you're the same as ever. Everything in rows and all white. Is it a complex?"

"I don't think so. I think I was born this way."

"Ruthie used to say I was an ink-blot sprouting cigar ash.

Couldn't stand me." It was an accurate comparison: he sprawled in the armchair with his tie askew and often missed the ashtray.

This was not, however, the kind of disorder that pained Alexander. Things broken and out of their places upset him, and leaky taps and stockings dripping: ash could be vacuumed.

"I hear," said Ziggy, "that the gold-rush is coming to an end. Both your mother and Mrs. Challenor have given up the struggle to find you a wife."

"I hope so."

"Working on a new book?"

"I'm doing the index."

"Yourself? Christ, man, what you need is a round little blonde graduate student. Let me know when you want to come up for air and I'll take you around to meet some people. It's time you got out of that goddam Harvard-Oxford-Westmount ghetto."

Ziggy disappeared for the summer, and Alexander flew to London to check references at the British Museum and attend conferences, but in the fall, finding himself at last with free time, he started dropping in at Ziggy's apartment, where he was liable to meet women of all colours, habits and descriptions, most of whom considered him a reactionary because of his family connections (which were not disguised by his surname) and discussed him unflatteringly to his face. One night, among them, he found a gaunt American poetess named Amaryllis.

She was as tall as his sisters, but differently made, a walking skeleton with large joints and a lantern jaw. She had the hollow voice of the buck-teethed, and tight, straggly blonde curls, and a great mat of blonde hair on her arms and legs. Ziggy told him she was mad as a hatter; that she had finished at the university but had not been able either to face graduate work or find a job. "She's bright enough," he said, "but undirected. God, can you imagine anyone focusing that and sending it all off in the same direction?"

She talked fast, but the hollow voice seemed to run behind the mouthing and the gestures, to come from a speaker somewhere else. She seemed by turns naive and supremely wise; she had great, haunted china-blue eyes.

AMARYLLIS

The next day he went with some trepidation to buy her book of poems at Heinemann's. As he was picking it out, the bookseller said, "You'll find that the girl is very good, I assure you." This frightened him. He saved the book until after dinner. (He cooked for himself, and with finesse.) He found that Heinemann was right, and fell in love with Amaryllis.

She was the child of American eccentrics of good family who had chosen, after *Walden,* to live in the country, and off the land. She had had a queer, isolated childhood, backwoods Maine alternating with expensive boarding-schools, and still seemed unsure what to do in a city. When he took her to restaurants she spilled her soup or her wine. She got very drunk, very fast. He found himself adoring her words, and entertaining her more and more in his apartment. He then prudently rented a larger one (she was all right if the pieces of furniture were far enough apart, otherwise she knocked over his little Knoll tables and bumped into bric-a-brac). When he found that she wasn't actually living anywhere, only with this friend or that, he asked her to live with him, and, at the end of the year, they decided to marry.

His mother, surprisingly, took to her, though she was annoyed when the engagement received large notice in the *New York Times,* for in addition to the sin of being an American, Amaryllis had committed the solecism of being a pedigreed American (the notice was sent to the papers out of some dim memory of her mother's about how things had once been done) with a list of ancestors beside which Alexander's family looked *nouveau riche,* and was.

They were married in the Cathedral between Eaton's and Morgan's, Amaryllis wearing her great-grandmother's yellowish lace and satin, which was not too small. Alexander's sisters attended her and Ziggy was best man: there was a six-inch discrepancy in height between the men's and the women's sides at the altar.

For the first year of their marriage, they went about in a trance. They were both lonely people, and now they were committed to keep each other company. They liked many of the same things, although Amaryllis did not entertain — indeed, she neither knew nor cared about entertaining — she was superbly active, she took him out of himself into sections of the city he had never before penetrated. She fitted into every milieu and did surprisingly well with the academics, and exercised her lively mind on films and plays. Her French was good — indeed, she seemed to lose a good deal of her awkwardness when she translated herself into the more feminine language — and she took him to parties where by himself he would simply have been another Westmount bastard. When they were home alone, he did the cooking. He kept his cleaning-woman, and thought that Amaryllis did not notice when he re-made their bed, to smooth the creases in the sheets, which hurt him.

About the time when he was beginning his first draft of the third book, however, she became pregnant. She was very sick, and after that, very sleepy. She spent all day in bed surrounded by kleenex and newspapers and basins and trays and could not be shunted into the winter cold. His mother and his nanny came to visit her, and, nodding wisely to each other, began to buy for the baby. Amaryllis read Dr. Spock in bed and asked him to make love whenever he passed the bedroom door. She phoned a department store and ordered nursery furniture, then discovered belatedly that they would need a bedroom for it. They moved.

The baby was born in the spring. She called him Tod. Alexander, irritably hoping to be able to spend the summer on his book, noticed that though she spent all her time with him, she rarely changed him. He was, furthermore, although a well-dispositioned baby, inclined towards projectile vomiting. The house, which neither of them took much interest in, began to smell.

When he suggested that his elderly nanny come to help, she was angry, and he discovered that she held firm and clear ideas on the subject of child-raising. Tod was not, she insisted, to be turned into a fussy child. Everything was to be nerveless and casual, the child was not to be sacrificed to the furniture or the upholstery; if there were sacred objects he should move them to his study upstairs.

Amaryllis-mother was not the same person as Amaryllis-poet. He consoled himself that most men make the same discovery about their wives, he was involved in an extreme situation because he had married an extreme woman. His work load, however, increased the next year, and it was disheartening to come home to no supper. She learned to scramble a decent egg for Tod, and often made the same effort for him, but the sight of Amaryllis with a paring-knife was unbearable, for she was as uncoordinated as ever, she could barely change Tod without swallowing his pins, so that he went on having to do the cooking, and since the cleaning woman had left, the vacuuming (Amaryllis and the machine together suffered from a plethora of elbows) and he phoned the baby-sitters as well because she hated to leave Tod, and by the end of the year he was fed to the teeth with marriage.

Tod was a beautiful child, with his mother's fair curls and his father's neat limbs; but he was also a child: he cut up a paper Alex was preparing for the Learned Societies, he rose early and poured ink on the white rugs. Amaryllis began to look guiltily at Alex. Alex began to glower.

"Why don't you write poetry any more?" he asked.

She did not know, she said. It had something to do with freedom. You wrote poetry, if you wanted to write good poetry, when your mind was free, and she did not feel free any more. But she warned him not to take it out on Tod.

They went north with a tent that summer. It rained all the time. Amaryllis began to have fits of crying.

When they returned to Montreal, she went on crying — everything seemed to be beyond her. "You should try not to," he said "it frightens the child."

"The child, is that all he is to you?"

"Tod, then."

"You never make love to me any more."

"You're always asleep or accursed."

She began to cry again.

"You ought to see a psychiatrist."

Then she exploded. "Is that what you think, Alex? Do you think I'm crazy because I'm unhappy with you? Is that your solution? Neither Toddy nor I have been able to put a foot right for a year. Whenever you look at us a martyred smile crosses your face. We're your cross to bear. You don't even speak to us, you just go around tidying up after us. Why don't you admit you can't stand us?"

He could make no such admission. He did love them, but in such an environment — in the mess, in the stifling hurly-burly of their childishness — he could express nothing.

A week later she took Tod to visit friends in Toronto. She never came back. Alex sold the house and moved his tattered goods to an apartment.

He made vagrant efforts to stay in touch with them, sent them money, sent friends to see that Toddy was well taken care of, sent her new books he thought she would like. Legally, he supposed, he might have assured the return of the child to him, but he could not part them. He went on with his work, feeling empty and failed, and taught in a small mumbling voice, and was neater and neater.

Amaryllis wrote him several long letters saying she still loved him, explaining the basic disjuncture of their souls, saying Toddy missed him. After a while he heard that she had gone to live with another poet in the country. When she asked for a divorce, he made it easy for her, and, as she had asked, put away money for Tod's education.

Ziggy Taler was digusted with him. "You let a good girl go without even putting up a fight."

"I suppose I don't like fighting."

"I know, it's not neat. You're turning into an old woman."

"Perhaps I always was one."

When the Separatist movement began to make itself seriously felt, he left Montreal. He belonged by birth to the other camp but Amaryllis and her friends had destroyed his loyalty to it. He did not feel that there was a place for him in the city except as an example of the dying vitality of the WASP strain.

He went south, across the border, and taught at a mid-Western university. The change invigorated him. He began to get his confidence back. His new book on international relations made him a minor celebrity.

When he was offered a job at Toronto, Toddy was eight years old. Alex found that Amaryllis was still living in the country, and had put out two books that he had not seen. He accepted the position.

AMARYLLIS

Soon after he settled in Toronto, he met a girl very like himself, admirably suited to him: clever, neat, quiet, serious. She knew Amaryllis; she had in fact edited her poems. She agreed to marry him, but did not wish to have children, for her career was well established, but not adaptable to long interruptions. She thought, however, that it might be good for Tod to come and visit them in the school holiday.

Except for a blank meeting over the divorce, when they had not been themselves but dry papier-maché lawyers' puppets, he had not seen Amaryllis for over six years. He drove north to visit her now, following a map she had sent with a cordial invitation.

They were living on the stoney scrublands south of Algonquin Park, along a dirt road that seemed miles from anywhere. Her map was inaccurate, but the village post office knew them well, and directed him. It was afternoon when he drove up their corduroy lane.

Tod, a thin, brown lad with his own face, stopped him half way. "She's chopping wood, mister," he said. "We don't interrupt her." Axe-blows fell far apart in the distance, ringing in the clear country air. "Are you Alex?" the child asked. He nodded, and Tod took his hand.

They walked up to the house — a cottage with unpainted board-and-batten siding — when the sound of the axe had stopped. Amaryllis came out beaming, carrying a baby.

He saw her with an awful surge of devotion. Living so much outdoors had consolidated her, she was brown and fat, her faded print blouse was pushed out at the buttons. "Well, Alex, this is Sabina." The baby was fat, too, and ruddy, far different from the waxy infant Tod. He smiled weakly at her.

"Bill's in the woodlot — Tod, run and get him. We're getting the wood in for the winter."

He looked around him and for the first time noticed the blazing autumn colour.

"Come in, I'll make you some tea."

The main room of the house contained a woodstove, a crib, and a big pine table surrounded by ladder-back chairs. One end held a collection of instant-coffee bottles. "I'm putting up jam," she said. Then, "I like it here. It's the way I was brought up, you know. I'm sorry I couldn't manage in the city."

"I'm sorry I couldn't either."

"I hear you're marrying Sue. She's exactly right for you."

He was too unhappy to answer.

"We make wine, too. Here, this is Bill's elderberry."

It tasted like cough medicine, but it cheered him, or at least cleared his throat so that he could speak again. But as he opened his mouth there was a commotion in the lane.

"Oh Lord, it's the CBC, they're filming us to-day. Who'll I say you are? Do you know anyone there? Can I say you're from my publishers?" She handed him Sabina, who began to cry, and then barfed on his shoulder.

Tod and Bill — a bear of a man with a black beard got up to look like a voyageur — came pelting out of the bush. Tod took the baby from him, Bill pumped his hand. "I hear you want young Tod for the holidays.

"If he wants to come."

Amaryllis called out, "Alex, is the cabin tidy?" and dashed in through the screen door. "Oh hell, it looks like us, anyway. They can come in." Alex made his excuses.

"It's the worst possible day," she said. "Come again, will you?"

He made his way back to his car past men with cords and video cameras.

Tod came at Easter, since they had agreed by letter that the roads would be too difficult at Christmas, and quietly submitted to expeditions to the Museum and the theatre. But at night he sobbed in his sleep and called out for Amaryllis and Sabina.

On the fourth day Alex asked him if he would like to go home. He said, "Yes please," avoiding his father's eye. He packed his own suitcase in the neatest possible manner.

Alex left him at the bottom of some frozen lane and thought that he wouldn't see him again until he was embarking for some foreign war.

TRANSFORMATIONS

HAVING been told that it was the highest virtue to see herself as others saw her, Lou learned in the company of the elegant to feel shabby, in the company of the shabby-genteel to feel worldly and slight, in the company of boys her own age to feel hairy, and with girls to feel inferior. She was only really comfortable with two of her mother's sisters, Floss and Ruby, who, in spite of their foolish names were warm and looked on her as a kind of miracle, which she then became. But of course they died.

Still, she managed to grow up and consider herself less damaged than some of her friends, whose view was from a single facet rather than the whole crystalline structure from which she had achieved her perspective. Sometimes, indeed, she thought she had acquired the variety of Cleopatra: that was in her twenties, when her luck was good.

Time passed. She was good at her work, but she married. She would have thought herself an awful failure if she hadn't married. And she liked Dick, totally liked him. She didn't know what all that stuff they called love about about — she meant, she had thought she knew when she was sixteen and reading books like *Wuthering Heights* and coming home after dances, finding it too glorious to go inside, so, trailing her long, new New Look swayback fuzzy brown overcoat in the brown leaves, danced outside the house in the side yard for ages after Wallie Purvis left her shyly unkissed on the doorstep, until her mother, looking for all the world as if she was going to say "Oh husband, oh husband, the grey goose is dead," called her in.

The moon was high that night. They were living in a house with garlands of gingerbread on the grey gables. Wallie Purvis didn't kiss her but she didn't want him to. She was saving herself for better things. Yes, she knew about love.

She was never so certain of that again. She had loved one man at a distance so desperately that she thought she would die; when he came close up, she was ill. She had been loved in the same obsessive way; it gave her claustrophobia. She and Dick liked each other fine; they married.

They bought a clapboard house and filled it with old furniture from Floss and Ruby and his aunts; had children. She never told him that sometimes she felt like Cleopatra. He remarked that she never walked by a mirror or a store window without looking in it. Was she afraid she wasn't there? She thought he was kinder than her sister, who said she did it because she was vain.

She had three children; drove them to lessons in things; delivered Meals on Wheels; worked for the IODE. Finally, when the children were more or less launched, went back to work.

And turned forty, which displeased her more than she had thought it would. After all, what had been so good about all that shy agony?

She didn't tell anyone she had turned forty; it seemed unnecessary. They had all grown up together. Her body was still good, though soft in patches. There were bristles to be tweezed out of her chin, but never mind. Dick wouldn't laugh at them, everybody's got them. So far so good. She was forty, she had survived, if a few bristles were the price, well, then. . .

One day she found she couldn't thread a needle. She went to the little old eye man who was bent over double like a gnome, but ground a wonderful lens, the last independent. "What's the matter with you, Lou?" he grumped. "Turned forty?" She admitted this, and he cackled. "Happens to us all, one day, even the youngsters like you. You'll get to be sixty, too."

On the way home she thought of that and discovered that she had no urge to get to sixty. Forty, she thought in her heart of hearts, was enough.

But enough of what?

Their house they had bought cheaply because they loved it. Now, it was what they called a good investment, and now also that all the others had given their aunts' furniture to the Goodwill, Dick and Lou's furniture had to be registered against eventual capital gains taxes. They didn't want to do it. They hadn't bought it in antique stores, they had simply preserved it. But their accountant said it was the only thing.

She came into her lovely house and hung her hat on Ruby's buffalo-horn hatstand. Then she looked in the mirror and she wasn't there.

She looked again, expecting one of her faces to emerge from the clouded old glass; but in none of her guises was she there; there was no Cleopatra, no Theodora Droodge, no Pollyanna, no Anne, no Elsie Dinsmore — no Lou. No one.

I've already done it, she thought. But her fingers touched oak, horn, glass, metal coathook, their own dry selves.

I could swim out to the middle of the lake, she thought, the way we used to. Wallie would stand on the shore and wave like mad when we'd got to the horizon. Sometimes we only swam until the top of the flagpole disappeared. They said it was madness to do it without a boat, but we were mad — mad waterbabies who swam miles against each other.

I could swim out. I wouldn't know what happened. It would be easy, it would be soft. I would be so tired I would just go to sleep. Become part of the water. It wouldn't hurt.

Then she remembered it was only February. Swimming was out of the question. She put the supper on.

She liked her job, even if she wasn't there any more, not in windows or in safety glass or in mirrors. She went on getting up every morning, putting on her eye makeup, (because curiously she could see one eye at a time, for practical purposes, though never a whole face), driving the car to work, lunching with Dick, buying boots and shoes for the children, keeping things in order at the office and at home. Sometimes she wondered why, if she was so good at putting things away, she had lost herself.

She would have asked the minister, but they didn't go to church. She would have asked the local psychoanalyst, but she had known him when he was a lonely intern, disinclined to accept the sexual mores of young women locally and well brought up. She went on not being there. Dick said she looked pale, perhaps they ought to take an early holiday.

I know what I am in Dick's eyes, she thought: a wife. Then, "What do I look like to you," she asked.

"Why . . .yourself. A little older, of course."

"How much older?" She was surprised to hear herself speaking like a jealous woman.

"Oh, about two weeks," he said, teasing. He had worried when his hair turned white.

"You look like Cleopatra, sometimes," he went on. "Your hair so dark and cut straight; your eyes slant up now or seem to. Everyone says it's marvellous the way you don't get older. You do, a little, to me. I guess I have to make you older to compete with me; but you're looking wonderful, Lou, really wonderful."

She thought, that's it, time's been going backwards, I'm at zero again. Soon it will be time for swimming.

Spring was thunderous, but there was an election and they were both busy in it. Dick managed a campaign, she ran the office, the boys cut staves and put signs up. You couldn't say they weren't busy, involved people.

Just when she worried that the campaign would be over, she'd be idle, she realised how many things there were for her to do after work in the house. And Susie was in the orchestra: there were rehearsals to drive her to, and clothes to make. She hardly had time to look in the faceless mirror at all.

Once, when she did, she caught a glimpse, just a glimpse of herself. It was the bedroom mirror; she was rolling her tights up, thinking how disgusting they were, when stockings had been somehow graceful, though not the things that held them up; and she caught a corner of a stringy-looking thigh in the mirror, and turned away.

"You're getting too thin," Dick said. "You ought to go to the doctor."

She couldn't imagine going to her doctor about being too thin, he to whom ninety percent of the world was too fat. He would only congratulate her. Still, it was true she was thin. She had stepped on the scales that morning and found she had lost twenty pounds since she disappeared from the mirror. How very odd, she thought, and what an elegant cure of overweight; if I could market it I'd make a mint.

At Easter, they went to the West Indies on a stockmarket windfall Dick had made. Their children filled whole beaches with their exuberance. Dick was exuberant too, but she was not. The warmth and the rum made him lusty in bed. She found herself twisting and turning away from him, forcing herself to give in because she was foolish not to want him. She felt bad about it: it reminded her of the awful single years when you didn't go to bed with people because you wouldn't be marriageable if you did, and anyway boys weren't supposed to get what they wanted.

In May, just when the trees were coming out, she learned that her job was being consolidated away in some kind of reorganisation plan. It and she would soon cease to exist. They would make another place for her, though. "Oh, no!" she shrieked, as if she were afraid of mice.

The trees were greening. The children left for school very early. Dick left soon after. For the sheer luxury of it, sometimes she went back to bed. She could see the lake beginning to sparkle blue from her bedroom window. The leaves of the trees were such a tender green, the air was soft. She wished the house were still isolated so she could get up early and naked, plunge into the water. Now, the women from the subdivision behind them had adopted the habit of lugging their brats down to the beach at the break of dawn. There was no advantage to being a native any more, and a limit to her desire for democracy.

I wish the world was still a secret between God and itself, she thought.

She tried to go out more, because when she was with the children she felt brassy and bossy, and when she was with Dick she felt ordinary, which since she had disappeared was hard to bear. But there was a limit to shopping, she was no longer interested in the IODE and no one played bridge any more, even in the subdivision. She took to walking barefoot on the beach all afternoon, climbing around and over the groynes near town, then walking free, miles and miles further up, coming home exhausted.

Stray dogs followed her, children stared, but she walked and walked. Sometimes she was too tired to cook: she went out for ridiculously fried chicken.

"Would you like to move?" Dick asked. "Are you tired of this place? The kids would like Toronto or Montreal. New York, even. I could get a transfer to New York. Nobody wants to go there. We're here because you like it."

"No," she shook her head. "No."

"You've got to do something about yourself, Lou. You can't let yourself go to hell in a hotrod this way."

"Am I drinking too much?"

"No, of course not. I'm worried about you. You're just not yourself."

"How?" Could he see what she did not?

"Well . . . I can't put my finger on it . . ." he trailed off in his easy chair.

If you can't put your finger on it, what use is your finger? Cut it off. Then, if the world was an egg, I'd break it. Then, I'm sorry Dick.

"I'm sorry, Dick" she said.

"We used to be close. You're remote now, cold. You can tell me if there's something wrong."

He sounded like her mother when she said, if you get into trouble come to me. Which she didn't.

"No, there's nothing wrong. I just feel . . . forty."

"Oh, if it's only that." Who was forty-two.

She went on walking. Waiting for the water to warm up. It would be best to swim out from the old pier at Crinians, she decided, it would give her a head start. Meanwhile, the beach, which was eating away the shore, thus graced with collapsing willow trees, was beautiful and deserted and hers.

One morning she went back to bed after they had all gone away to work and school, then, restless, taken a shower and gone back to bed again naked and wet. She opened the window and let the wind play across her body and then was greeted by a stab of lust so swift and strong it was almost a pungent smell.

After that, she wanted every man she saw on the beach. She was a bleeding wound of desire to such an extent that it was a game for her, it was funny. She couldn't pass an upright branch of driftwood, let alone a suburban father in shorts playing volleyball with his four-year-old. The people two lots up had planted yuccas along the front of their property and the great phallic calyxes were thrusting up: my God, she thought, I'd do it with them too. Then laughed: it was shaming, but somehow good.

She didn't know what to do about it but keep her hands in her pockets and enjoy it. She thought of going to the psychiatrist after all, she phoned to make an appointment, they said they would call her back in a month, she decided not to. Then he called her. "Lou," he said, "I've had a cancellation."

He was different. Changed and dignified by his opinion of himself, by the things he had had to do. There was also something unpleasantly pretentious about him; he reminded her of ministers a church who took themselves too seriously, they were the Rev. Mr. So-and-So and too much loved; it must have galled their wives. "Lou," he said, sighing, "Lou, you never knew it, but I really loved you. You thought I was after your sweet ass, but I loved you; you turned me down, you were trained to. What's happened to you, Lou?"

She told him she wasn't there any more in the mirror.

He frowned. "That's serious," he said. "If it's true." He got up. He put his arm along, but not on, her shoulders and marched her into the bathroom of his suite, where there was of course a mirror. She was there. Her face beside his. Both of them looking not quite the people they once were, that long time ago.

"What does it mean," she asked, humble now. He had been trained to demand, she had been trained not to give, she knew what the past meant, now, but the present was the problem.

"I don't know. And I don't think I'm competent to judge. There's a new chap coming. I don't know if he's any good, but I'll let you know if he is. Listen, Lou, I'm not God, I'll help you if I can. Are you going to kill anyone?"

"Only me, and I've been putting that off."

"When you can't put it off any longer, I'll be there for you. But I won't take you as a patient. I'm not what they call disinterested. We grew up together."

"You grew up with everyone here," she said, bitter and

rejected.

"A lot of the people I see are murderers," he said. "I also see women who are compulsive cleaners. You, Lou . . . I just want to see. That is a bias. Do you understand?"

She did, and she didn't; she went away on the whole satisfied. She was there in the bathroom mirror at home: she was there, but she was not in the living room mirror at all. She phoned Ben and told him that. "Oh," he said in a voice that didn't tell her anything at all.

After that, when she walked on the beach, she took a hand-mirror with her. Sometimes she was there, but when she was not there, she sat down crosslegged wherever she was and coaxed her image back. She could coax and cajole it, she discovered, as if it were an angry but very dependent child. She would talk to it and praise it and flatter it, so that first one eye and then another, an eyebrow, half a mouth, a nostril, then the rest of it would flicker back. "I love you," she would say, "You are good, you are sweet, by nature," ridiculous things like that. "You see things and make me want to do things. You taste and smell and are."

She neglected the house. She let the children do their own things — which they did well. She walked and muttered and smiled, and sometimes, timidly, swam a little; you are never supposed to swim alone.

She found a little gully full of white sand, newly eroded. In the hot weather she nested there, coaxing her mirror and talking to herself. A little boy stopped by her, one who had been playing airplane on the beach nearby, flying and screaming, "The Whole Wide Wor——ald". "What are you doing?" he asked.

"Talking to the mirror."

"Does it answer?"

"No."

"They only do it on TV," he said wisely, and went away.

The cove was like a pair of arms with a soft bosom. It held her and graced her with warmth. One side was almost always high enough to shade her head. There were soft pebbles and bits of driftwood in the sand. Sometimes, when the waves had been high the night before, the lower edge of its triangle was damp. Then she wrote foolish things in the sand, "I love you, me," "When we were

young we were stupid," "I miss you, Ruby," "She never told her love," "For I myself must like to this decay."

The weather darkened, the water rose. Her cove was too small for her now: it was fall.

Dick said to her, "I don't know what you've been doing, but I've never seen you looking half so well." One eye, one eyebrow, a nostril, half a mouth, two moles.

Benjamin, at a party: "You've survived without me. I find I'm bitter."

She returned both of them the same feckless smile, knowing that she had not yet beaten plate glass windows.

ZIGGY
AND
COMPANY

HOME THOUGHTS
FROM ABROAD

RUTH was sitting with her sister Hanna in Finney's Restaurant waiting for Frank Rademacher. Hanna was talking. Hanna had been talking for four days. Her flat, nasal voice seesawed through a domestic chronicle Ruth had taken no interest in for fifteen years: the family, the business, the aunts, the uncles, the snobbish-sister-in-law, the delinquent nephew. The ups and downs of the hat business that were mostly downs. The stock market. The family. The business. The aunts. The uncles. Home.

Hanna was two years older than Ruth and looked ten. Her flat face had not improved with age. Ruth looked at her rancorously. They had never got on together. Why had she asked Hanna and Lou to stay with her? So they wouldn't go back and say she hadn't asked them to stay? Was she such a coward? She ducked under the flow of Hanna's river of talk and tried to amuse herself by looking around Finney's, the world-famous London fish parlour. She hated fish.

"I don't know who this Frank guy is," Hanna said, "but he sure is late."

Ruth ordered another drink. It would loosen Hanna's tongue further, but she felt a need to dim her own reaction. She had looked to her left and seen three large white boney women eating three large white plates of white boney fish, gelid and steaming. She had looked to the right and seen a famous fatuous television commentator consuming a crab. She had told Frank that she had

63

to entertain her sister while her brother-in-law was at a meeting. Frank had said to bring her along. "But Hanna keeps kosher," she told him. "Then we'll go to Finney's," said Frank, all suavity and perseverance. So they were in Finney's.

The restaurant was in an alley in the theatre district and had a reputation for its oysters, which were out of season. It was a proper British sort of place where fish was served as fish — steamed or boiled without benefit of continental disguises. You could have boiled mayonnaise with your fish, or green cornstarch-and-parsley sauce. Ruth, who was thin, and had never been interested in food, and was in the business of disguises (she was a theatrical costumier) sat with one hand on her glass and one on her diaphragm as if to suppress its revolted rollings. The smell of pure undisguised old-fashioned fish permeated the furnishings and fell out of the unfolded napkins, hung like a vapour over the rows of dated theatrical photographs that faced her. Frank was half an hour late and her only distraction now was the menu, which she could hardly bring herself to read, and Hanna's conversation. Across from her, the television commentator began to look like a heteroclite goon from Monty Python. After his crab, they'll bring him wriggling jellied eels, she thought.

Hanna went on and on. Montreal was better since Expo. Everybody was coming back to Canada now, everybody who was any good. Why didn't Ruth get married again, why didn't Ruth come home?

"No work."

"Oh Ruthie, there's lots of plays in Montreal now. New theatres all over the place. . ."

Ruth let her talk. No use trying to explain the world's workings to Hanna, to whom ten years' effort to establish yourself in London and Paris was simply a return to the continent of the gas ovens. Her father always used to say Hanna was like Aunt Gisel, which was a kind way of saying she was the family fool.

Of Ruth he had said that clever women lacked tenderness, or words to that effect. She didn't remember the kind of words he used any more.

Hanna asked her why she didn't get married again again, and who was this Frank character, anyway, and why didn't she want any kids, all she was doing was saving up for a lonely old age, and how old did she think she was, anyway, and Ruth was spared answering when Hanna broke off mid-banality and held up a rednailed finger: "Did you hear that, Ruthie?"

"What?"

"That voice. Behind us. I guess on the other side of the partition." Which she knocked with her knuckles. "There's another part of the restaurant there, eh?"

"Yes." The building was long and shallow, divided into crowded little rooms by thin brown wooden panels. Lots of little rooms for the waitresses to let their hair down into the soup tureens.

"Well, listen."

She listened. At first she heard only a babble of voices, then one distinguished itself. It was Ziggy's. For the first time in the day she smiled. She almost giggled.

"Get a load of that," said Hanna. "What would he be doing here?"

"Ziggy travels a lot," she said coldly.

"Yeah, I saw him on the TV one time last year, by satellite from some place in Africa."

"He works with gorillas now."

"Think he's got one in there with him now? Where's the powder room? Maybe we could sneak through and get a look at him."

"Good God, Hanna, why?"

"Well, aren't you interested in anything from home, even your ex?"

"I can see him on television too, you know."

Ruth and Ziggy were married when they were both nineteen, at the end of their second years at McGill. The reasons for the marriage now seemed obscure, unless they had to do with the fact that Ruth shared a bedroom with Hanna and that Ziggy had a classic Jewish mother, who was Ruth's mother's best friend. The triumphal prestige of getting into McGill had not lasted long — it was getting easier — neither of their families was well enough off to give large space to a non-earning offspring, and one night coming home from the movies they had decided to pool their scholarships and make a premature entry into the world. That meant, in those days, that they must marry. It had seemed like a wild adventure.

It was taken that way by both their families and the university administration, whose attitude was both paternal and maternal. They were advised that they were foolish children, and that their marital activities must replace extra-curricular ones. Ziggy was barred from his place on the university newspaper. Mrs. Taler and Ruth's mother fell out over whose child was responsible for the decision. Opposition crystallised resolve.

Married students were not unknown on the campus, but they were the first of the generation to marry, a source of novelty and nocturnal visits: culture heroes. They had fun and worked hard. The first year was like playing house.

Ziggy was studying biology and sociology, Ruth, English. They often audited each others' courses, they combined their friends. Their meals were midnight hamburgers, their stone-cold flat was a haven of privacy. At the end of the year when Ziggy went north to work at Chibougamou, Ruth missed him badly.

At the end of the second year of the marriage, they were graduated in an impressive ceremony on the lawn of the university, both with honours. The day was splendid: sun sucked the limpness from the new green trees, there were the scarlet doctors' robes, the marquee tents were gay. The federal politician who spoke, spoke briefly. They sang the Alma Mater and for a moment believed the words.

In the evening, in the kitchen, after the party on Park Avenue, Ziggy unveiled his five-year plan.

Ruth was to get a job, he was to do his Master's in Social Anthropology. This he could do in two summers and one academic year, he had been offered a graduate assistantship which would pay his fees and three hundred dollars a year. If Ruth worked for two years at seventy-five dollars a week, at the end of that time they could afford a baby, which Ruth's sister would look after while Ziggy did his Ph.D.

Ruth stared. "And what if I don't want to?"

"What do you mean you don't want to? Isn't this marriage a

co-operative effort?"

"Supposing I wanted to do my Ph.D.?"

"What good would it do you, three years of Spenser with Hemlow?"

"I'm going into the theatre, Ziggy."

"Listen you aren't going to fart around sewing for that West-mount gang."

"I told you in February: if you're going up to Chibougamou again — you said you were — I'm going to apply for one of the costume jobs at Stratford. I did, and I got it. I told you, you just weren't listening."

He looked at her blankly. "But I'm not going to Chi-bougamou."

"You'll just have to look after yourself this summer. I'm going to Stratford."

"The hell you are."

"Why not?"

"You have to stay here. You're my wife."

From that day on she ceased to be his wife.

He told his friend Alex about the quarrel. Alex was single and failed to understand how they could not have heard of each other's plans before. Ziggy ran through the list of his banned extra-curricular activities, and Ruth's: he had organised two demonstrations against rising student streetcar fares, written unsigned editorials for the McGill *Daily,* demonstrated at a series of evening-course botany labs, lectured at the Workmen's Educational Association and shingled his mother's verandah. Ruth had dressed four plays and worked part time in a clothing factory. "We were always studying," he said.

He believed for some time that she would come back to him, but when she returned to the city she took a room of her own and went back to work in the clothing factory. He saw her a couple of times on the street, looking thin and worried. She spoke to him tersely. He tried to soften her with blandishments — he was a short man like a teddy bear — but she only said, "Ziggy, I meant what I said, to hell with you." Finally he shrugged and went out to make new friends.

They heard of each other, of course. Ruth's mother and Mrs Taler were umbilically attached by their telephone. They were scandalised, worried, sick with worry. Hanna was sent to Ruth's room regularly to see what kind of trouble she had got herself into, and could find none. Ruth came home the odd Friday night for dinner, but could not be persuaded to return to Ziggy. When she made up her mind, she was a stone.

She had a big soft cousin named Sheldon who was a lawyer, and had always been fond of her. She couldn't afford the divorce (a private bill to the legislature, it had to be, in those days) and for a while thought of moving to Ontario, but Sheldon got it for her in the end — put it through with a pile of others, robbed the rich to pay for the poor. Ziggy made no difficulties: was tired of living alone. Ruth didn't ask for anything but her freedom.

That winter she met on the street a blonde girl she remembered well from McGill, a zingy little cheerleader type with big breasts called Rosebud Morrell. She looked at her once, smiled, looked at her again and remembered that she had heard once that Ziggy was going with her. Yes, this was the one: Mrs Taler had been complaining about the possibility of Ziggy and the goya. It was a cold night. "Let's go in for coffee," she said.

"I've only got a minute."

They sat in the restaurant booth until the steam wore off their breaths. The hot coffee hurt Ruth's teeth.

"Late for something?"

Rosebud, who was not usually so shy — she had been known as the girl who made the animal noises in the back of the lyric poetry class — squirmed and blushed. "I'm going to the rabbi."

"Whatever for?"

"I'm being converted. I'm marrying Ziggy." She wore a camel hair coat and instead of gloves, hand-knitted mittens. Ruth looked at her hard and decided that in spite of what Mrs Taler thought, she wasn't rich. She was from Ontario, not from West-mount and her cashmere sweaters looked like hand-me-downs. She weighed her like a chicken with her eyes, decided that Ziggy would like her very, very much and said, "Don't look so scared: it's no business of mine."

Rosebud blushed again. "I've got to go, now. I don't want to keep him waiting."

Just the wife he needs, Ruth thought. And then: who the hell would have thought of Ziggy marrying a woman named after Orson Welles' sled?

She picked up the twenty-cent check as a wedding present. Shelly had given her a divorce for a wedding present. "Mazel tov," she said.

She found herself grinning as she hurried along the opposite side of the street. It was a good line, the one about the sled. Ziggy would laugh like a drain. . .

She thought that one through and decided that living alone was having no one to tell your one-liners to.

She tried to tell it to Shelly in the spring. They were sitting in the sun on the stoop at home. Her mother was at Ziggy's wedding on the invitation of Mrs Taler. Ruth could not help feeling that this was disloyal, but she knew she would want to hear about it, so she had come home to sit around waiting for the full description. Shelly came over. They had an odd conversation, beginning sentences and not finishing them. Finally Shelly said, "To hell with it, Ruthie, what you need is some good booze and a good bang, a coupla days in the Laurentians. I'd take you myself if I didn't have to show up at court to-morrow morning." His hand crept out, and she held it listlessly for a moment, and then said, "Stop, Shelly," and ran away to spend the rest of the day at the System scratching through four movies.

Shelly died of cancer of the liver a year later and all the family said how they knew why he never married and looked at Ruth.

Ruth looked at her watch. Frank was an hour late. Not like him. "We'd better order," she said.

"Would you mind if I just sneaked around the corner and had a peek to see if it was him?"

"Yes."

"I'll have a prawn salad, then."

Ruth ate brown bread and butter and watched Hanna work her way through a mountain of shrimp and some cress that looked as if it had been grown on the premises.

"You always were a snob, Ruthie."

"What's that?"

"The way you're looking at me."

"I thought you kept kosher."

"How'm I supposed to know prawns are shrimp? Anyway the place was your idea."

"Frank's. I hate fish."

"So do I, frankly. I don't know who your friend is, but. . ."

"He's a business acquaintance, actually."

"And he phones at midnight? Some business."

"Theatre, darling. He knows I'm home then."

"You should get married again. You're getting a pinched look, an old maidy look. Anyway, the theatre's dying."

"So they say."

"I guess I'm coming on too strong, but I guess you didn't see that television show about him."

"Frank?"

"No, Ziggy. Not the one in Africa, the new one, showing him on his estate in the south of England: great big house — don't know what you'd call it, French provincial maybe — and this jeep that he runs around in, the back seat full of gorillas. And his new wife. She's not so pretty, well, she's attractive, but kind of plain. You know, the sort that if she swallowed a gumdrop she'd turn into an ordinary hausfrau like me."

"What happened to his second wife, for goodness' sake?"

"That was the funny thing about the programme — I mean, the whole thing was funny, Ziggy wearing one of those little Tyrolean hats with a backseat full of gorillas in Tyrolean hats, and he's got a whole bunch of assistants in overalls with some kind of crest on them, you say Montreal is full of jumped-up phonies but you never see anything like that. Anyway, he's talking away about his work, very important research he says it is, to me it looks like those movies they used to make with chimps, and he says his wife helps him, she's the business head; only every time he refers to her he says, "my new wife", so finally the TV interviewer — English, you could tell by his accent — says, "What happened to your old wife?" and Ziggy, he hasn't changed a bit since he was six years old and into Aunt Yetta's purse, he said quick as a wink, "She got fat!"

"Oh really, Hanna."

"He did. He said that. For a minute, I was so mad. I thought, the nerve of him, he looks like the bear who got into the honey himself, the nerve of him, he looks just like his Uncle Abe that worked in the cigar store. And then I thought, well, gee, that was Ziggy. He never bothered to tell a lie, and I decided maybe it was okay after all. A lot of men leave their wives when they put on weight and give long complicated reasons. She was the type, too, she had that white, white skin and the blonde hair. What was her name, something funny, Honeybunch?"

"Rosebud."

"Migod. She was a good wife, too. Mrs Taler taught her to cook the way Ziggy liked it."

"Oh come on, Ziggy's idea of a real good time was to sneak off somewhere and eat pork chops."

"Well, he certainly didn't keep to the rules, but she did, and she was so clean you could eat off her floors. She had the four kids bang bang bang all in a row, she kept up with the family. She still brings them down from Toronto for Seder."

Ruth slumped in her chair. "He's a bastard, Ziggy."

"I don't know, Ruthie: a man with that much energy, maybe he needs four wives, or four different kinds of wives at different times. Rose was a good woman, but she let herself go. I guess it was all she could do to look after the apartment and the kids on the kind of money he was making then, and I don't think he ever had any real liking for housewives. Maybe he wants perfection, maybe he'll get it, who knows? Have you read his books?"

"Only the one about gorillas."

"You should read the first one, the one about how there were wonderful women in primitive tribes and the strain died out when the city was invented. It seemed to be all about you. I laughed till the tears ran down."

"I didn't know you read anthropology, Hanna."

Hanna shook herself free of the last of the cress and the shrimp. Ruth ducked as a platter of steamed turbot sailed dangerously past her nose. Hanna said, "I can read, Ruthie. Maybe you never noticed; besides, I have to keep up with my kids."

71

"What are Ziggy's kids like?"

"I don't know, now. I saw them a couple of years ago at Bernice's: three beautiful little blonde boys and a red-head girl the image of Ziggy. I wish that friend of yours, business or personal, would turn up; didn't you make me a hair appointment at three? Is it far away?"

Ruth looked at her watch and felt a hand on her shoulder She twitched convulsively. She had been very far away. Man? Dead man? Gorilla? It was Frank, full of apology: nothing but delays, last-minute telephone calls, traffic jams, and just on his way here being literally dragged into the Blue Posts by that damn Irish actor he was trying to get for the new production which he hoped, "Ruth. . ."

Ruth said, "Hanna, this is my sister Hanna, she has to be at Sloane Square at three."

Frank's eyebrows flew up as if they were on springs. He wants something, she thought, now he's scared he won't get it. He said, "You're not looking well, Ruth."

"She doesn't like fish," said Hanna. "I was going to try the desserts but all they have is pudding. Where do I get a taxi?"

"Hanna, it's quicker by underground."

"Not for me, I always get lost; you know me, sister bird-brain."

"I can go around to my garage and get the car out again," Frank said sincerely. He was lighting a cigar.

Ruth packed Hanna up and took her over to Leicester Square to find a taxi. "Do you think you can find your way back to the flat or shall I come for you?"

"Maybe I'll walk for a little while after, and then take a taxi. Listen, if he asks you out for dinner or anything, don't worry about us. We can take care of ourselves. Maybe there's even some-thing to eat in that dinky little fridge of yours, eh?"

"Got your key?"

"Sure, honey. Have a good time. I like a man who smokes cigars."

Ruth walked down narrow streets to the restaurant and stared through the window at Frank for a moment before she went in to join him. He had lost some weight, he was dealing with a glass of wine and a lobster. He was tanned, but two white worry-lines showed between his eyes.

"Sorry," she said when she sat down.

"My fault entirely."

The buxom waitresses were packing the restaurant up around them and making a noisy job of it. The last stragglers had taken their seats at the matinees. "Do you want to talk about the show?" she asked.

"Never talk business when I'm eating. Could've shot that bastard O'Reilly, wanted me to drink Guinness on an empty stomach and damned insistent he was about it. So that's your sister. Married young? Grown up family? Husband in business, doing well?"

"I suppose you could say that."

"Trouble was, I was about to ask you for a weekend in the Cotswolds before I saw you had a duenna. Wouldn't do now, though. Trouble is, you have to have lived in England for four years at least before you like that sort of place. Miles from anywhere, nothing to see, nothing to do, three-room cottage with a wine cellar and a cupboard full of tins and jars from Fortnums. I've had Americans there, they always want hot water. Woman comes in Friday morning to light the Aga but you couldn't run a shower."

"It sounds super."

"Does, doesn't it? Someone told me once a man who smokes cigars isn't supposed to like solitude. More for a pipe type."

As he talked, he cracked and clawed at his lobster. Waitresses shook out tablecloths around him. He bit, chewed, spoke again. "You don't look enthusiastic."

"Oh, but I am. I love being alone myself."

This was not the conversation she had meant to have with him. He was talking the way he talked to actresses, not . . . he reached out and put a big hand over hers. "We'll do the show," he said, "if that's what you want to know."

"Don't you even want to see the sketches?"

"Good God, I only spoke to you about it on Tuesday. Don't you ever sleep? Do you need the work so badly? You know I wouldn't work with anyone else. There's no one to touch you in the business."

Stolidly, silently, he finished with his crustacean. He called the waitress and was annoyed to find that Ruth had settled her part of the bill.

When she got into the street again she took a deep breath of air and found she was standing under the restaurant fans. She swayed against Frank's arm. "Steady on," he said.

They sat for half an hour in Leicester Square staring at Shakespeare's statue. Sheepish, worried, half-joking, he offered her a penny to spend in the underground loo if it would help. She shook her head and sat just close enough beside him to feel the warmth of his comfortable bigness. When she was able to speak, she said "Let's go."

In his big grey car he said, "I'm taking you to the country. Don't worry about clothes. Enid left half a dozen pullovers and some trousers last time she came down. You can ring up your sister and tell her some rigamarole."

"Thanks."

"The rest will do you good."

She fell asleep part way through the hassle of getting out of London, then woke suddenly because they were somewhere in the country on a gloomy lane. Frank had stopped the car and was leaning over her, looking at her closely. His face seemed as big as the moon. "I thought I knew you," he was murmuring, "I thought I knew you."

SUBLET

A lemon-faced judge said "By virtue of the powers vested in me by the Criminal Court of Canada, I now pronounce you man and wife." They sniggered. They had decided to get married in the spring; but the wedding was postponed by a delay in Ziggy's divorce papers and then by the summer course he was giving in California; and then by existential hesitations, because sometimes it seemed a pity to spoil a longstanding and satisfactory relationship by legalizing it.

One Monday morning in October, however, they both arrived blushing, with seconds, as for a duel, at City Hall, to commit themselves to each other permanently.

In the evening, although they had not intended either to celebrate or publicise the event, they allowed a Greek friend of Ziggy's to give them a party in his restaurant. There was a bouzouki band, there were cases of champagne. Friends came at short notice. They had a wonderful time, and felt vindicated.

"I thought I wouldn't like it," she said on the way home, "but I did. No one made vulgar remarks about brides. It was marvellous, wasn't it?"

"Mmmmm," said Ziggy, locking her in a half-Nelson. "Bit of a skirt in a taxi. Mmmmm. Wonderful."

"Who was the little bald man with a fringe of white hair? Was I supposed to know him?"

"Toto somebody. Lives with Marina. She's away. Mmmm."

"Never liked Marina. He seemed beside himself with altruistic joy."

"Mmmm. Like that, Toto. Free champagne. Here we are. Carry you up?"

"Good God no, Ziggy."

Ziggy was a social anthropologist who worked with gorillas, whom he was said to resemble. He was short, and thick in the leg, and barrel-chested. Hairy. And energetic. This week, he devoted his energy to his marriage and lectured with his eyes fixed on a farther, delicious shore. He was home earlier than she was, and spent his time fixing surprises for her, and unpacking the wedding presents that began to arrive from her relatives in the west. And inviting friends to drop by. It was like a week of birthdays, until she took her rent cheque down to her landlady on Friday evening.

Then a storm burst: it was a respectable house and now look what had happened: doorbell ringing day and night, telegrams, parcels special delivery; no peace in the house and all that singing on the stairs; all the wax off the front hall. Wedding presents! Mrs Pritchett was shocked by the noise over her head . . . It was one thing to have Dr Taler there on and off all these years, but now to get married and make noises about it: they could find somewhere else to entertain their noisy friends.

Ziggy rolled screaming on the carpet when he heard: "The wages of sin are collected when you repent." He took off his sweater and scratched his huge hairy torso. He banged his big feet on the floor. Mrs Pritchett below rapped on the wall. He gargled with laughter and banged his feet again.

Barbara looked around and wondered how these little rooms had previously contained him. They would need a larger place at any rate.

They had thought of staying in her apartment until they had saved enough to buy a house but the truth was they did not have much money. Ziggy had child-support to pay from a previous marriage, and she was subsidizing her mother. She started to house-hunt during lunch hours and after work and asked Ziggy to do the same. He asked hopefully around the university and left the rest to her.

One night near the end of the month she was packing alone.

SUBLET

Ziggy had grown irritable with the subject of moving and had gone to a movie. It was fair enough, she supposed, since most of what he called (when he was asked to help pack it) "the guff" was hers: he kept his books in his office and lived out of a suitcase otherwise. But she was staring glumly at the "Apartments to Let" columns of the Saturday paper when the doorbell rang.

It was the man they called Toto come to pay his respects to their nuptials. She asked him in for a drink and hoped that Ziggy would be back before he left.

He was an easy guest: he settled comfortably into an armchair and talked intelligently about Ziggy's latest book, about the university, about his friend Marina. He asked her what she did and said it sounded interesting. He told a story about a film-maker he knew. When she asked what he did, he said he made films too. He had come to it late, of course, he wasn't one of your young whippersnappers with a Super-8 from school and a headful of acid and Marxism, but . . . yes, come to it from advertising — dreadful world that, called creative, but no room, no freedom there — and he was getting on nicely, now. Experimental techniques in animation, you know.

She wasn't sure she knew. He explained that by scratching the emulsion of film — directly on the film — there were results you could get, striking, like Klee. Of course, Norman MacLaren was the pioneer, but he was with the Film Board, he had a reputation, a wide piece of leeway. Toto was on his own.

The explanation lasted until Ziggy returned, glad enough to see the visitor who fends off the marital quarrel. He broke out a wedding present bottle of Crown Royal. They grew convivial. Finally Toto said, "I hear you folks are looking for a new apartment."

"Yes," said Ziggy, with his tongue drawn back defensively.

"Well you know Marina's gone to Mancelona for the winter, her mother's not well and she figures it's a quiet place to get some writing done. And I'm off to Sausalito to make a film. You can sublet our place."

She was watching Ziggy's face for his reaction. Ziggy licked his lips.

The next night they went to Toto for drinks. "Not Crown

Royal," he said, as he handed round glasses of beer, "but you know, I'm on my own in this business. . ."

It was a wonderful place, an enormous two-storey studio off an alley, the main room partitioned off with flats and stage-props (she remembered a little theatre group playing in a place like this ten years before) dominated by a huge bed on a dais. The kitchen was in the corner of the main room, an electrical island. There were paintings stacked on the open rafters. Toto said he was through with paintings but they helped against winter drafts. Downstairs there was a primitive bathroom next to Toto's workroom; and next to that, the overflow garage of the neighbourhood bread company.

Toto warned them that the place had its disadvantages: the drafts, the early-morning noise of the trucks, but the rent he named was reasonable and they went home pleased as children. Just their neighbourhood, so big that Barbara's furniture would fit in without being noticeable, and Marina, who made macrame as well as poems had hung the place about with knotted curtains that made it look like some kind of magic cocoon. It struck Barbara that the huge scale of the place was better for Ziggy: her little old-maidish attic cramped him. They phoned Toto, who said he would not be leaving for San Francisco until the 15th, but they could move in now.

"I don't know why we weren't more suspicious," Ziggy mourned later. "It's the goddam third time I've been married, I ought to know something about life."

"We were high," she consoled him. "High on getting married."

Toto brought a pick-up truck on Saturday and carried Barbara's Victorian love-seat down the attic stairs as if it were a balloon. If he dropped her grandmother's sherry glasses, she agreed with Ziggy that without him they would have had to pay large sums to a mover and it was certainly easier with three than with two.

That night, she cleaned the kitchen stove (Marina seemed to have been away for a long time), discarded the leftovers from his refrigerator, and made them an elegant supper to go with the

Nuits St. Georges that Ziggy had laid in. Toto was pleased.

And the next night they invited Toto as well, because it was Sunday, and the casserole could be shared, and he was looking a little lost, a little dispossessed. In gratitude, he knocked at the door at half-past eleven and asked if he could make some hot chocolate in the kitchen; and this he garnished with whipped cream and presented them with on a tray in the regal bed. Since it was really his bed, it seemed rude to ask him not to sit on the end of it. He unlatched a guitar from a hanging screen and said, "Here's a song for honeymooners."

He did not play the guitar very well, but his voice was light and gentle. They lay back dozily and thought, how pleasant, and then, doesn't he know any short ones?

A routine developed. She had to be out earlier than Ziggy: the whole of the flat's facilities were hers while the men snored. Then Toto would go up to the kitchen at half-past nine and make Ziggy and himself instant coffee. They would chat a while, and Toto would do something useful and domestic — dusting or vacuuming — all the while dragging out objects and explaining them to Ziggy, while Ziggy readied his notes for his lecture at eleven. In the evening, because it was only until the fifteenth, they found it easier to share their meals with him than let him putter around them in the kitchen. He was self-effacing about the bathroom.

No doubt, then, that he was good company. If his folksongs were too long (he took them through the history of folksong from the Irish balladeers to Buffy Sainte-Marie via Pete Seeger and Joan Baez and he knew all the verses) his stories — of people he had known in the movie and entertainment business in London, Paris and Toronto — were amusing and when they had friends in they invited him up if he was around. And he was always around.

She tried re-arranging some of Marina's objects and replacing them with her own, but Toto always noticed, and she was embarrassed to feel she was a usurper. She grew impatient, and Ziggy reproached her. "Communal living's the thing, hon; you're too territorial. Let the poor old guy get what joy he can out of us."

At breakfast, he took to reading Ziggy his poems: sketchy assemblages of rebel sentiments on thin, yellowed wartime paper.

SUBLET

The fifteenth came and went. Toto kept to himself for a few days and emerged for supper later, looking worn and elderly. He would have to stay on, he said: his contact in San Francisco was still away in Japan. He left off folk-singing, and they were much relieved.

"What does he do all day?" she asked Ziggy.

"I dunno: bustles around, I guess. First he makes my coffee, then he does your housekeeping, then he reads my paper. Is he here when you get home?"

"I generally hear him humming in his room when I go to the bathroom."

"He's pretty good about the bathroom."

"There's that."

One night she came in tired from work and explained that they would be eating out. He said he was glad to see young people having a good time, and after that they often found a sign on their door, "Sorry folks, out to-night. See you to-morrow."

One night, lying in bed beside a snoring Ziggy (she was subject to attacks of insomnia when she was short on sleep), she tried to summon up Toto's face. She could not. The shape, yes; but she could not envisage the details. She struggled to draw them until she fell asleep.

Next night, she invited him to supper for the purpose of observing him. He had a round face, a curiously bland face. Pink, tufted with white hair, the eyes perfect pale-blue circles, the eyebrows arcs. His nose was round, too. He would have looked like Santa Claus, but for all his white hair he had not a wrinkle.

Ziggy started work on a new book late in November: rose early, covered two work tables with his cards, and exploded violently if he was interrupted. She explained the need for isolation to Toto as well as she could, and said, no, there were no errands to be run. Toto scraped and pulled his absent forelock to such an extent that she felt sorry for him and bought him a hotplate for an advance Christmas present.

After that, when they invited him for dinner, he implied that he had eaten better in his day. And the flat was shatteringly cold. When they complained he said he would see the landlord, but failed to reveal the landlord's name.

SUBLET

"The bastard," Ziggy said, "the slimey bastard. Here he is eating our food and there's no heat coming out of the registers at all. If we move the furniture to block the drafts, he complains about it. And do you realise the phone's been cut off? Either he goes or we go."

They came to an arrangement: Ziggy would go through the bills with him, and pay enough on them to get the telephone back and fuel oil delivered again. Ziggy would even look at his film to see if someone he knew might. . .

Suddenly, Toto announced that he was going away.

This left Ziggy answering the door to process-servers. When Toto returned in January, the refrigerator and the television set were gone. Toto was sulky: he said what you did when they came was give them something on the account, the loss was unnecessary. However, if he could raise the cash he was going finally to San Francisco, but he had one final request. An important friend was coming to see his film on the seventeenth . . .

The studio was turned back into a studio again, Ziggy's work-cards banished to a cardboard carton; she tidied the place, and laid in beer for him; Toto moved through the room the evening before distributing his possessions artistically. Ziggy got him a projector from the university, and they accepted an invitation to friends.

"We're not ourselves," Dick Pargiter said when they arrived. "But we're still alive. And he's gone, isn't he Lil?"

Lillian sank back smiling with a glass of gin. "You men are cooking to-night; not me; not by a long shot; not me."

"We're celebrating the lifting of a feeling of oppression," Dick explained. "Osmond's gone out."

"Osmond?"

"Osmond is Lillian's cousin. Osmond is in films. Osmond has been living with us for months, years, decades, aeons, eternity. More gin, dear?"

"Send out for pizza, Dick."

"For company?"

"Ziggy's not company. Send out for pizza."

Barbara shifted awkwardly, hoping she was not going to witness a family quarrel, but Dick began to giggle, and poured his wife another drink, and went to the telephone. "I hope you don't mind," he said. "But you have to open the valves sometimes."

"Oh, Osmond will cope to-morrow. What else has Osmond got to do except think about his bloody movie? At least he's good with the kids. I'm going to drink gin until it runs glugging down the side of my face."

"It won't be long, dear."

"I don't care. Osmond's gone out. Do you hear that, everybody? OSMOND'S GONE OUT."

Where had Osmond gone? Ziggy asked.

Osmond, they said, dear, sweet, fey, feckless, hungry cousin Osmond, had met another film-maker.

Barbara sat up. Stories began. They fell into each others' arms with laughter over the pizza.

When they got back, weak with laughter and drink, Toto was still entertaining his guest with tales of the rudeness of the world to creative enterprise. The younger man looked starry-eyed, impressed. They climbed onto the high bed and began to undress. "Go home, Osmond," Barbara said. "They need you for to-morrow."

Ziggy lent Toto fifty dollars towards his ticket for San Francisco. He said he was disappointed in them, but he left. It took Ziggy weeks to straighten out the financial picture, and he resented the loss of time, but once the heating system was repaired he said it was the best place to work in he had ever had. And when they were alone together again they felt as joyfully guilty as they had when they were living in sin.

In the spring, Marina returned from Mancelona. "You've cleaned up the place," she said.

"We have," said Ziggy. "I guess you'll be wanting your books."

"They're not my books."

"Your curtains."

"They're not my curtains." And then, half-wistfully. "I never knew who he was, or where he came from. He was boring, but he knew how to look after people. He's dead, did you hear that? They wouldn't let him work in Los Angeles, the bastards, and he starved to death. I sent a hundred and fifty bucks towards his funeral."

SUBLET

They gave her his guitar, and a few mementos they had found around his room—postcards, Paul Rotha's film book. She was moving on to Montreal, she didn't want the paintings, she said. She took two suitcases from the rafters and went away in a taxi. Ziggy said he didn't see Toto starving to death and the funeral ploy was the oldest in the world. Barbara wondered how he could be so callous.

She was depressed for a week, Toto was always in her mind. He had been kind and charming; he did all he could to earn his living. Ziggy was so cynical, it went with being Jewish and studying gorillas, human values did not matter to him, not the way they did to a minister's daughter. She went to a movie, and in the dark, she wept for Toto.

Coming out, she met Martin Anselm and went out with him for a drink. He said she was looking glum, she told him about Toto and how Ziggy was unkind. Martin laughed. "Come on, I'll show you his memorial."

He had a movieola in his working-room. He wound a film through. "It's Brian Viget's, he lent me a print of it. See that room?" He stopped the frame for her, then turned the handle again. "See that group at the party?"

The room was rather glorious, almost as good as theirs— handsomely decorated, off-beat. The group around the coffee-table plotting revolution included Toto.

"So you're living in the place on Euclid, are you? You didn't see *Dead Lively* did you? Your place is in it. It's Philippe Arsenault's studio. Toto's the guy who rents studios from painters who go away on Canada Council grants and rents them cheap to film-makers for arty party-shots. You can dry your tears, Barbie. This scene wasn't shot more than a month ago—on Spadina. Toto's still around."

The strip of film was used later to clear Ziggy of a charge of pawning Arsenault's paintings. Toto got off lightly, he was frail-looking and polite to the judge. Ziggy took Barbara to Africa with him. He said that after Toto she wouldn't mind gorillas.

WHAT DO LOVERS DO?

CATHY was a great reader, as they said, and, coming from where she came from it was not hard to identify with the heroines of the Brontë sisters. She would have given anything to love as wildly as Catherine loved Heathcliff or as despairingly as Jane Eyre loved Rochester, but though she fell in love often enough, the men who responded to her were not those she loved. In her finest wild Yorkshire Moors mood she frightened men away. Her love affairs usually had to do with real estate.

She had been in love with Laurie Power and Malcolm Magee and — and —: the thought of them now still gave her a wonky feeling in the throat and a twinge for her young unknowing self. The first man who slept with her was her boss at the Hydro office, and that was about getting a lawyer for a piece of land she wanted to buy. The next one was, in retrospect, a good fellow, a superior lover: who wanted to buy her land from her. After she quarreled with him she went through a morbid stage of parading herself in a then outlandish bikini on the beach and accepting all comers; but she had not been raised to do that. She agreed to marry her next serious lover, to bury guilt in domesticity. Two nights before the wedding she found him poring over plans to develop her bit of land.

So that she was left with unfilled expectations and a ticket to Europe. Her mother, who was practical, said she would return the wedding presents if Cathy would go to Europe alone. She had money in the bank, time on her hands, why not? She could meet some other girl in London or Paris and travel with her.

She got off her honeymoon flight at Orly airport alone. With her map and highschool French she located the hotel her French teacher had recommended and rented a room. She went to bed at 8 and got up at dawn to explore.

She was not a good traveller. She did not think she would ever be. She had always hated leaving home. Neverthless she struggled with the cobblestone streets and closed August restaurants of the Left Bank, because she had read about them. She knew where Sartre lived in Ste Germaine des Prés, she stared through the iron gates of Gertrude Stein's courtyard, she crossed the bridges to the museums and art galleries.

No, she was not a good traveller. She wore a long conservative navy blue raincoat and brown Oxfords. She looked twenty years older than she was among the minidresses of Paris. She was ashamed of herself and frightened of the city.

She went to the Louvre on a Wednesday, trying to find an Egyptian collection she had seen floodlit on a magic Friday night. She got lost. There was hardly anyone there. She saw the guards staring at her as she glided in her rubbersoled shoes from room to room. She felt older and dowdier each time she saw them staring at her. She seemed to be stuck in 18th century furniture. She decided she hated 18th century furniture, except for celestial and terrestrial globes. A long way back there had been some heavier, more mediaeval-looking stuff that was better, but now, alone, with the guards staring at her, telephones ringing when she entered a room, guards muttering indecipherably to each other, she hated gilt chairs and puffy pastel tapestries. She hated the way the guards were looking at her. She decided she was paranoid, the adventure was too much for her, she had better take the next plane home.

Then she entered a big room like a throne room and one guard turned to another (putting down of course his inevitable telephone) and said in perfectly understandable Grade 10 French "That is the woman who touched the inlaid table." Her knees melted but she managed to ask him where the exit was.

Paris, she decided, was a bust. She had a railway pass and a list of the museums she and Jack had decided to see together. She

85

buried herself in Flemish painting in Belgium; there was a Van Gogh show in Amsterdam, a sculpture exhibition in Copenhagen. She went to Stockholm because she had always wanted to. It was a lonely way to travel, but she resisted the impulse to give her lonely heart away. She stayed in the museums until closing time, ate a modest supper, went to bed early in innumerable hotels. How could you see a foreign city in the night?

Oslo confounded her. Oslo was full of rain. She could not find the paintings she wanted to see in the art gallery. Her money was running low, so she was staying in the Youth Hostel, from which she had to be absent between ten and six.

Sunday was her third day in Oslo. Her shoes were wet and squelchy, her raincoat was permanently out of shape and her hair had bunched up in little ringlets in the damp. She went with a bunch of students to a sculpture park and decided that she disliked monumentalism in the rain. Descending from the park, famished and cold (it was mid-September), she discovered that in Oslo on Sunday, restaurants did not open until the minister of their parish had descended form his pulpit. Hungry and enraged, she took a streetcar to the main square and decided to spend the last of her crowns in the Opera Cafe.

It was a grand, glassed place that overlooked the statue of Ibsen. It was warm. The menu was in French and English as well as unfathomable Norwegian. She had been making out on a pin-point system heretofore, and had had her fill of beans and boiled fish. She ordered herself the meal she should have had the courage to command in Paris: oysters, consommé, quail. To hell, she thought savagely, with folk parks, Viking ships, museums, rain. She ordered French wine and a green salad.

She swallowed her oysters and her soup. She was cutting up her quail when she felt a man looking at her. A short, stout, curly-headed man. He came over to her table. "Are you left-handed or Canadian?" he asked.

She forgot that sex was misery and asked him to sit down. She said that she was left-handed and Canadian and starving. "That I could see," he said.

His name was Ziggy. He was an anthropologist from Montreal. He lived in England. He was in Oslo giving a paper. She said it was a miserable place. He said it wasn't if you stayed in a good hotel. She told him about the youth hostel and her wet feet. "Tell you what," he said, "I'm free tomorrow . . . would you?"

Monday the sun shone like the gold in the Swedish flag and she met him under the clock of the new town hall. There was a parade, and everything was gay. They drove out to the suburbs to see the Viking ships in their white stone chapel, and stood and worshipped ancient things in silence. He took her hand.

There was something about him not like any of the men she had known at home: he laughed in bed.

On Tuesday they set out at dawn to drive overland to Bergen. She had cashed her railway ticket to contribute to the gas money. They drove over mountains and dashed down the sides of fiords. She read the guide to him so he wouldn't miss any stave-churches on their way. They stayed the first night in a youth-hostel with box-beds and eiderdowns and rain. On the way to Bergen they visited Grieg's tomb, in the rain, again. He was holed up in a cave in the side of a rock by the water. He said "It looks like Muskoka," and squeezed her hand.

They ate fish in Bergen and had tea in a glassed-in Konditorei on the second floor overlooking the harbour; and went into the Hanseatic museum and found it tiny and possibly unchanged since the day the League moved out: dusty undisturbed clerks' ledgers, dried fish, quill pens. They put the car on the ferry to England.

It was his birthday. They had wine for dinner and went out on deck in a raging gale. "Lash me to the mast," she cried.

From Newcastle where the streets still had Scandinavian names he drove her through the Brontë country on the way to London. He apologised that he could not linger, he had business in London. They agreed to meet in the north of France in a fortnight, and chose a little town from the Guide Michelin.

In London, she missed him bitterly. She felt she had been missing him all her life. He was fun. Still, he had his work to do, and probably a wife to deceive. She had no illusions about him. Somebody who liked women that much couldn't possibly be free.

After Scandinavia, England seemed dirty and mean. She had a list of Cathedrals to see and went down to a radiant Salisbury sitting in a flooded water-meadow and then, on impulse (she had crossed 9 out of 10 plays off her London list), went to the south coast and took the ferry to France. She would go to the Proust country and wait for him. She owed herself a second crack at France.

She was getting short of money and knew he had to be careful of it himself. Therefore, in a town much smaller than Illiers, she took a room in a hotel over the pool-hall for four francs a night. The place had once been a coaching inn and was a maze of outbuildings, one of which advertised the fact it had once been a Cinema. The proprietress was ancient and dried and brown, had a cataract in one eye and had had a Canadian lover in World War Two. Which made up for the fact that the wallpaper in her room was cascading down.

On the fourth day of her stay she took sick of an overdose of cider and cream. A doctor was called who said her liver was pre-ternaturally damaged by an infant diet of milk. She was yellow, she vomited, and, surprisingly, she cried. He gave her injections of hormones and advised her to drink herb teas.

She had never in her life been ill before except annually, on July 1st, from sunstroke. She had never, in her mother's busy household, had time to be sick. You just didn't malinger in bed. Here she did not malinger; when she got out of bed, her knees folded.

Madame's daughter, a dour forty-year old with pursed lips who didn't think much of foreigners but kept a close eye on the games machines and the pool table, looked after the cafe, and Madame looked after Cathy, bringing her books, vervain tea (for the liver), and company. The Canadian lover, a soldier from Trois Rivières, loomed large and lonely. Madame took a coy and fluttery look when she spoke of him, as if she and the wallpaper paste had never dried.

After a week, Ziggy wired that he would be late. She decided it was just as well. That day she had tried to venture out to the main square and nearly collapsed. Anyway, at the drop of a hat, she cried. He wouldn't like that.

Theoretically, the hotel did not serve meals, but Madame brought her broth and herb tea on a tray. Eventually, Cathy found the energy to ask how much this would be, and was astonished. She wrote home to her mother for money. Saying she was ill, but not seriously.

The day Ziggy came there was some kind of village fête, and Cathy was sitting groggily under a striped umbrella sipping weak French beer (because wine, tea, lemonade and coffee were forbidden and she didn't know about Vichy water) when she saw him. He looked like a fat leprechaun, she decided, but also a little older and more responsible than in Norway. Something was weighing on him. Time, perhaps.

He put his arms around her. He sat down in the square and clapped his hands for the waiter. He rushed her to the hotel, was charmed by it, left his luggage, dragged her out to the festival again. Urged her to eat, was crestfallen when she explained her illness, stalked up to a trailer selling cheeses and nosed along them; bought cheese and sausages and wine.

He had maps, he had plans. "This will be our most wonderful holiday," he said.

She had tried hard not to count on him. They were half-way down a little river going to the sea. When he said "our" she sat on a stone and cried. He looked at her with very great patience. She knew then that he had children. "Come on, try," he said.

There were two little towns at the mouth of the tidal river. Big Port St Pierre on one side, Little on the other. The Big Port was cold stone, grey and hostile. For 10 cents they took a rowboat ferry to the other one, where immediately they found a cafe and ate fresh sole, dandelion salad, and fried potatoes, all of it exquisite. She hadn't had such fish since she was up north with her Uncle Austin and he caught bass.

On the way home she turned yellow and vomited. She shivered in the evening damp. "I'm a mess, I'm sorry," she cried.

The next day he got up at dawn, and she slept late. She found him working on lecture notes downstairs. "This place is a gas," he said, "but I could do without the old woman's chatter."

There was a tower he wanted to climb. She sat at the bottom of it, panting and feverish. He thought anyone who could drink French beer—and would, in preference to cider—was peculiar. They didn't get along.

WHAT DO LOVERS DO?

She thought of him afterwards as the dearest, most impatient man she had ever met; then remembered the terrible dreariness of putting in the days. She couldn't eat, she couldn't drink, she had not the energy to explore. He was faced with her bare lackadaisical self and he didn't enjoy it.

She knew he had sent himself the telegram and was annoyed that he thought her stupid enough not to recognize the form. She parted with him gently, without bitterness — he was not the sort of man you could possess — and, she thought, well, nicely. She made no claims. He was her first lover who hadn't wanted her land. Her failure had been one of liver and enthusiasm. Liver failure provokes failure of enthusiasm. He had spoken, anyway, inadvertantly of a wife. She waved him off almost as if she was his mother.

Her mother sent a hundred dollars. She settled her bills, parted mistily from Madame, and went to Paris. The air was autumnal, but the restaurants were open. She discovered her French was now good enough to order in modest restaurants and when she explained her diet — "pour le foie" — and ordered vervain tea, she was treated with respect. She bought an antique map of Alexandria for thirty francs from a dealer around the corner from Joyce's house and went contentedly home.

BREAK NO HEARTS THIS CHRISTMAS

CAROLYN woke up early and remembered it was Christmas day. She knew, somehow, that Ziggy had already gone out. She must subconsciously have heard him stoking the coal stove in the kitchen, or wakened a little at the sound, and, remembering her childhood—the sound of her father's shovel grating against the cement cellar floor of the coalbin—snuggled down again.

As usual, she could see her breath in the bedroom air. It was supposed to be healthy, but she would never like it.

She swung out of bed and scooted around the corner to the loo. Pulled the chain, waited for the whole thing to come down. As usual, it didn't. The Best Niagara held. Good old England.

That first, friendly thought passed quickly. England might be all right but not this goddammed cottage. She hit her head on the usual beams going down the stairs. She thought bleakly that it would have been better if she'd put up Christmas decorations. All they had was a knot of holly on the mantelpiece, and a few cards. She disapproved of cutting down trees and it was silly to keep Christmas for Ziggy, who was not Christian.

The kitchen was warm. The stove was a real Aga cooker, right out of Elizabeth David. The kettle sang at the back of it. Thank you, Ziggy. She made herself a mug of instant coffee and settled, hunched, on a wooden chair beside it. She was bad at waking.

I'm glad he's off with the livestock, she thought. How would

I be with children, slamming things around, moaning and groaning at the sight of their shining morning faces. Ziggy's bad enough. Up with a bound, betimes.

She wished she had a copy of the Toronto *Globe and Mail* to hide behind. Never missed it in Africa, she thought, nor in Cambridge. Miss it here. She felt like bringing her fist down hard on the Aga and burning herself.

They had been living in the cottage for five months. It was the real thing: thatched and draped with roses. It came with Ziggy's new job as curator or whatever you call it of Lord Philip Mountfoxford's goddam tame gorillas.

Ziggy had been so excited by the prospect that she had caught his enthusiasm at first. He was always such a kid, that's what she liked about him. He bounced and enthused and enjoyed. He had been studying gorillas in Africa, and lecturing on them at Cambridge and about to return to Canada when Lord Philip came along with his offer: a cosy cottage, a family of five endearing gorillas to superintend, unlimited prospects for research. A very small salary but of course half the royalties on the book they would do together.

She had wanted badly to go home, if only partly because she was mad at having her plans disrupted, but when she saw Ziggy's face, she gave in. It would be like depriving a kid of his toy.

She looked up the Mountfoxfords in Debrett's. They both had triple-barrelled surnames and idiotic pedigrees. It would be like living inside an English novel, which was, after all, her field.

Alas, Mountfoxford's estate, Grange Hall, was no Garsington. The architecture was good enough—it was a splendidly classical place with galleries and terraces—the lawns were old and green as guaranteed, there was an aviary and of course the gorillas' quarters—a converted labourer's cottage considerably better than theirs—but no one came down for weekends. Carolyn drove back and forth from Cambridge for a while, finishing her work there, and wondered if they would ever see the Mountfoxfords again. He had seemed all right. Tall, fair, enthusiastic, not at all chinless, even though he did speak with a mouth full of marbles.

The summer was pleasant on the estate. She worked on her thesis, cooked, got to know the village shop-keepers. Ziggy taught himself to drive Mountfoxford's Landrover on the curved, pink asphalt lanes of the great property, and developed absorbing — too absorbing — relationships with his grinning charges, who were delicate. They often had the vet for drinks. He was keen on emigrating to Canada.

In the fall, when she had finished her thesis and was finding time a little heavy, she looked out one morning on a parade of station wagons: the Mountfoxfords arrived *en train* from wherever it was they spent their seasons. Mountfoxford, Lady Amanda, or whatever her title was, a nanny in a cap, the Hon. John, the Hon. Philippa, the squalling Hon. Sarah. My English novel, she thought.

Mountfoxford and Ziggy took up with each other quickly, and, united by their mutual love for the gorillas, spent most of their time together. I must find something to do, Carolyn thought, I'm above these petty jealousies.

She was not inclined to crochet. The weather was foul. The smell of mildew pervaded the place. Ziggy said she didn't open the windows enough. She went to London and bought herself cobwebby pink woolly underwear of the sort her ancient aunts had worn, though lacier, and stacks of books. She should have been happy, she told herself.

She had not expected to make friends with Lady Amanda, whose picture she had seen in the newspaper. A swinging little number dressed in the latest. She had Ziggy and Carolyn to dinner and said not a word at the table; whenever anyone addressed her she picked up a book of matches, lit one, shook it out, smiled wanly and went back to looking bored. "Amanda doesn't take to strangers," Mountfoxford said as he walked them back to the cottage in lieu of offering port.

Carolyn was cross with herself for not having been able to accept this adventure in good grace. She knew that in her heart she was snubbing the aristocracy. Why Amanda should like the gorillas any better than she did, she did not know, but, as Ziggy said, she was unfair when she said Amanda neglected her children. Amanda did as she was bred to do, sit and look cool and beautiful, and sometimes she even noticed the baby when the nanny put it in her lap. "You're hostile," he said, "and for the most rotten provincial reasons, Carolyn. You're judging them as if they lived next door to you in Maypole and didn't go to church."

She was surprised to find herself asking him, quite in Amanda's tone of voice, if he'd mind if she went up to London for a while.

"I wish I could go with you," he said, "but we're starting the photography this weekend."

"I wish they hadn't given you that goddam uniform. You look like one of the gorillas in it."

Ziggy scratched his round, endearing head. "They always say people take after their pets."

She would have liked to make love to him then, but Suzie Q. was sick and he had to go over and give her her medicine.

She went to London in a rage, stayed with friends who found the Mountfoxfords hilarious. Victor Newburn, whom she hadn't seen for years, took her the rounds of the bookstores and the pubs beside them. She felt warm and good-natured.

When she got back Ziggy was relieved. "Thank God you've come, we're bidden to a dinner party this evening. Some old zoological duke. It will be like a scene from a comedy."

It was not.

She felt martyred and furious. "Listen," she said, "I've no life at all, you're treating me like an old boot, I've nothing to do here."

"Stop talking like a spoiled kid. It won't last forever."

"Well," she heard herself flashing, "Neither will I." And went to bed crying.

They had always had an agreement that their work would come first, before anything else. She had found this pleasant and practical. Other times, other places, she had been left entirely on her own and had loved it, but here she could not keep her temper.

It seemed so foul, so silly. "They're dumb people living in a dumb way," she screamed at Ziggy. "For him, his children don't exist. He only likes the gorillas. She's crazy. She never does anything but comb her hair, light matches, or complain. It's sick."

"It's my job. Why don't you try to find some way of getting through to Amanda?"

First Suzy Q. had the colic, then Betty Grable. George was

far from well. Bertram and Gertrude had to be carefully watched. It was hoped they would mate.

She asked Victor Newburn down, so she had someone to talk to. He helped her with the washing-up. She fell in love with him.

She felt heartrendingly disloyal and guilty. At the same time, still angry. "Why do you do this to me?" she screamed in her head. "Notice me. Notice me."

"I'm such a bitch," she said to Victor when she was in London. "I've been able to hack everything else but I just can't take it on the estate. I didn't mind the gorillas in Africa, though I didn't see much of them either; at least I didn't mind being just put down. I never felt abandoned. But you know the other night I woke up and he was snoring and I shook him awake by the shoulders and said "I'm here" and he just went back to sleep again. He's exhausted. Gertrude's in heat and he sits around waiting for the males to attack her and they never do. I think it's the fact that they wear clothes."

Victor grinned. "They're better to hear about than live with, that's what it is. They wouldn't let you use their library, the Mountfoxfords?"

"They haven't got one. I don't think they can read."

"You are bitchy. Let's go out for a drink. You ought to get away. You can come with me to the Near East in January, if you like. I'm doing a lecture tour."

She turned him down nicely and went chastely back to the country. Ziggy appeared not to notice that she'd been away. Bertie was responding nicely to hormones, he said, and Suzie Q. had learned to ride a tricycle and was a menace on the paths, she had better watch out when she was out walking.

Fury met her whenever she looked in a mirror. She sulked and fumed. Could not stop herself. In the afternoons, after she had coped with lunches and sculleries, she took long walks in the damp beechwoods behind the cottage, where the grey trees had eyes and eyebrows and sometimes comforted her. She wished she would meet a prophetic old man on a stile who would tell her what to do. She wished she could throw herself down on the leaves and cry, or go home (though she had no home) or at least not bitch in her head all day.

"You're a mess," Victor said, "you'll have to get out of it somehow. I wish you'd come with me. I don't want to carry you away forever, I want to put you out of your misery — or pull, rather."

"Ziggy," she said, "I really can't take any more of this."

"I told you," he said coldly. "It's my job."

"I never see you any more, so what's the point of staying here with you?"

"It's only a few months. I usually see you in the morning."

"I can't focus in the morning. Look, I know you think I'm a poor sport, but I think I'll go up and stay with the Ratchetts in London."

"Carolyn," he said, turning his solemn eyes upon her, "you married me."

"It appears," she said coldly, "that I married a vacuum."

"Well, what the hell do you want?"

"Company!" she screamed.

"If you go," he said, "don't come back."

When she thought of their quarrels now, she found them almost classical, almost comical. They were playing roles foisted on them generations ago, using old dialogue and rusted routines. He accused her of jealousy, she accused him of neglect.

"Well," said Victor, "if you're fascinated by gorillas I suppose it does take the heart out of anything else. If you still want to come to Israel, I hope you'll leave your handwringing behind you. It's not you, you know; not the you I remember. Ziggy's no fighter, either: surprising what people do to each other."

She thought of staying, she thought of going. She felt weak, divided, disgusted with herself. She lay in bed beside a snoring, inert once-athletic man and thought, "Damn it all I have loved you!" Dying for him to wake up and tussle her into forgiveness.

She was less in love with Victor than she had been. That feeling was a first, sharp stab of a desire to escape. Still, she liked his company. Company. She was nervous of going to bed with him but she supposed if it didn't work out they'd still go to bookstores together. Anyway, it wasn't to be a marriage.

She looked at Ziggy on the pillow. The much-married, and

now I know why, she thought. That wonderful enthusiasm — for how long. I could go back to my old job in January. I should write to them. No, get a bit of sun with Victor first.

Ziggy was placatory for a while. She let the weeks seep by. Went to dinner at the big house again, again was snubbed by Amanda. Who spoke to Ziggy. So that's how it was. Not that it mattered.

She told Victor she would come with him. Decided to leave off telling Ziggy until after Christmas.

Now, Christmas morning, she huddled against the kitchen stove, miserably drinking instant coffee, wondering whether to start bacon and eggs. I don't want to leave him, she was thinking, I don't want to leave him, but I must. He's turning me into a termagant.

He came in softly, handed her a ribboned box. In it was a cashmere sweater, the colour of one she had admired on Amanda. She found him her love-gift: a shirt like one of Mountfoxford's. We're just beastly little provincial snobs, she thought.

"I'll make the breakfast," he said.

"No, I will."

"It's Christmas. The least I can do."

"Okay, go ahead."

"You look low."

"I'm getting a cold."

"Gertrude's down with one. That's the awful thing I have to tell you. The vet's off and the staff's gone, so, noblesse oblige. Guess who has to spend Christmas dinner in the monkey house."

"Oh Ziggy!"

"We're supposed to go up to the big house, but if I go, Phil will have to . . ."

"Blast Phil!"

"Well, it's my job."

"I'm not going up there by myself!"

He stood stock still by the stove, staring at her levelly. His eyes looked strange. "No, I didn't suppose you would. Where are you going?"

"To Israel. With Victor." She threw her head on the table and began to cry.

"Well, that's it, then, isn't it?"

The bacon and eggs were never cooked, because the cook had fled. She ate a piece of dry bread, then packed her suitcase. Half an hour later, she was walking through the beechwood, wondering if there were buses on Christmas day.

The woods were still, silent, full of fog. She understood English myths: these trees could surely walk. Way, way up in the sky, far away, a faint sun tried to gleam. Her footsteps scuffed the leaves. She thought, I've failed; no, he's failed; no, I've failed; if I were any good I'd go back and sit with him in the monkey house. They'll send him his meal on a salver. I shouldn't be doing this. I feel as if I'm dying, but I never die when I feel like that. I should go back. I won't. Let him come and get me. Let me carry out all the cliches, I'm human.

At the edge of the wood she saw an old man and a boy cutting holly.

Almost as soon as she got to the stop, the London bus came. So that was that.

NATIONALISM

ZIGGY, having at last found a sailing, embarked from England, endured for four days the company of a libidinous lawyer in his cabin, and slept enormously (he was not one to drink beef tea on deck all day), sailed home down the St Lawrence. The rough tree-coloured shores reminded him of silk-screened Group of Seven paintings in banks, and then didn't. Anticosti loomed, with its mysterious appealing memory of geography books and submarines and war. It was a brilliant day. He clung to the ship's railing and stared lasciviously at his native coast, pretending he was Rousseau.

Although he had been listed with several writers who were returning from abroad to savour the joys of nationalism, he did not consider himself a writer except occasionally, and he was returning for his own reasons. He was, like his friends, a patriot when it suited him, an opportunist otherwise. Lord Mountfoxford had sold his gorillas, his appointment at Cambridge was finished, and there was a vacancy for a social anthropologist at one of the universities in Toronto. He hated flying. That was why he was standing at the magic railing drinking in the glory of a season he no longer felt compelled to call autumn. It made him feel small and childish and pathetic, watching the scarlet and golden trees and the harsh rocks sail by. He though of getting off at Quebec City, rushing onto the train to Montreal, yelling, "Hey, Mom, I'm home." But she was dead and his father had gone to live with Aunt Florrie in Chicago. Ziggy stood alone, blinking like a returning soldier watching the shore coiling past him like a painted pythoness. He was forty.

England had and had not been good to him. He had lectured at Cambridge, and valued its society. He had lived free in a cottage on the estate of Ben Mountfoxford, observing the behaviour of Ben's gorillas, Suzie Q., Betty Grable, Bertram and George. Romped with them in Adam drawing rooms, Elizabethan galleries and Anglo-Indian arcades. Sometimes he rode beside Lady Amanda in a specially designed green uniform as she, having left her own babes squawling in their nursery, chauffered the gorillas wildly around the estate in a monogrammed Landrover. He had studied the unvaried intercourse of the gorillas with a view to helping Mountfoxford with a book. He had found their relationships boring and their personal habits disgusting, though he liked Lord Ben.

While he was at Cambridge or occupied with the gorillas, his wife had taken advantage of their relative prosperity to finish her Ph.D., an essay begun many years ago on lady travellers in the Middle East. Then, forgetting the retinues these doughty women travelled with, she had attempted to duplicate their feats. This resulted in amusing letters from Sicily, Greece, and Lebanon, and a fatal car crash in Israel.

He took no pleasure in the fact that she was buried in the promised land. Of his wives, only she had been good company. They had quarrelled before she left. To go to Israel a Jew attempting to bury there a Christian wife was to encounter both religion and politics at their worst.

When he returned to England empty, genuinely bereaved, and cynical, Lady Amanda announced that she was fed up with gorillas. Lord Ben, who had never stuck to anything for more than a year in his life, agreed that they were tiresome. As Ziggy drove them to London to the Zoo, the Long Gallery was already being redecorated with looking glass and silver paper. The gorillas soiled their crested blazers with ice-lollies and clung to him sloppily at the parting.

He felt himself funnelled down the St Lawrence, a ghost of aberrations in the past; aged, silenced, pressed from behind by legions of hopeful adventurers.

NATIONALISM

When he got to Toronto he took a room in a hotel, arranged his office and his schedule, and rented a car. Documented the changes in the city since his last residence there, gloomily approved them. His students, who had seen him on television programmes purchased from the BBC, were disappointed. He laid his finger characteristically alongside his nose, but did not joke or grin. They thought him dull, and sometimes booed.

Rosebud found him in the St Clair subway station, swooped and scrooped. She had remarried, yes, that was all right, but perhaps if he met Jake's psychiatrist . . .

He said he was in no shape to meet anyone's psychiatrist. He reminded her of the times in the past when he used to take the boys for weekends and Aaron hated him. His ex-wife brought a familiar bosom near to him and cooed. He went.

The psychiatrist looked at him coldly. What was he doing here?

"Being a victim," he said. "And what kid doesn't have problems at thirteen?"

"Ziggy's been working with gorillas," Rosebud said.

He stood up and shook himself. He found his heavy overcoat too much to bear. "I'm not married to you any more," he said. "It is nine years since we were married to each other. I am not part of Jake's family. I am part, perhaps of his complexes, and certainly of his heredity, but it isn't realistic to have me here. You've seen me now, I exist. If I can help Jake, I will. I'll take him out on Sundays. But you wanted those kids untainted by me and I agreed to go. I have gone. Goodbye."

Wondering if they were going to come and get him with white coats.

He walked home through the market and stood for a long time staring at the brown crisp carcass of a roasted pig in a butcher's window. He saw a figure reflected in the glass. "You are thinking racial thoughts," he said slowly, separating the words.

Alex North laughed and put his arm around his shoulders, reaching down to do so. "Come for a drink," he said.

Alex's wife Sue was in Bermuda attending to her ailing mother. They lived — how un-Canadian, Ziggy thought — in the same white gable where he had left them 5 years ago. "You look depressed, Ziggy."

"I am."

"I shouldn't wonder. Where are you living? I've been trying to reach you at the department."

Ziggy shifted in embarrassment. He had not been returning calls. Why, he wondered now. My oldest friend.

"Listen, this woman I know called Theodora — no, it isn't a plot — has asked me to dinner. She's a marvellous cook. It will take you out of yourself."

Theodora was big and dark, half English, half Spanish, from the West Indies. A surgeon who taught at medical school, a friend of Sue's. And indeed a marvellous cook. Her boyfriend was a hilarious story-teller. For the first time in months, Ziggy laughed.

At Easter, Jake's psychiatrist asked him to take the boy for a holiday. Ziggy explained that he had no holidays, the psychiatrist said that Rosebud was disillusioned with her marriage — that bouncy dream of her childhood to be a brilliant wife and successful mother had punctured once again and spread foul air on the most sensitive son. There was also the matter of competition with the elder brother.

Ziggy took an apartment. The child changed schools, and after the original week's nervousness, appeared to be getting on well enough, though he was passive and quiet. Then the principal phoned and said that he had grown violent. "When? How?" Ziggy asked. "During a sensitivity session he assaulted his teacher." "A what?" "A sensitivity session." "Christ," said Ziggy, and grew violent, and withdrew the child, who did not need training or encouragement to be sensitive.

This encouraged Jake, who immediately became more friendly. They waited guiltily a while for the truant officer, but no one came. Ziggy bought Jake a sketch book, a note book, a handful of Pentels and each day gave him lunch money and admission to the Museum, hoping he would not buy drugs with it. In the evenings, they read quietly together like a pair of recuperating invalids.

Term finished early in May. Theodora drove them up a road they had never travelled to her house in the country, and left them there for a month.

NATIONALISM

The land look alien and ungroomed after England. It didn't seem at first to suit them. The house sat firm and plain a hundred yards from the dirt road in the middle of the field. The barn was rented to a farmer who came every day in an old Chrysler to look after his stock. When they wanted food they had to bicycle to a nearby village. Ziggy rode the female bicycle because Jake wouldn't.

Otherwise there was nothing to do until Ziggy found the fishing rods and discovered that the mysterious black line behind the barn was a cedar grove on the slopes of a creek. They stood, batting black flies and mosquitoes amongst lacy cedars in Theodora's rubber boots and general store jeans, knee deep in marsh marigolds, fishing for trout, and twice catching them. They were not healed, but they were occupied.

Jake found a bird-book and learned waxwings from robins. Ziggy wrote down the gorillas. They lost their timidity and ventured further afield on their bicycles, using Theodora's survey maps. Jake asked Ziggy to tell him the different kinds of cows and laughed when Ziggy couldn't. Ziggy taught Jake to cook and used up all of Theodora's curry.

In June, the weather opened out. Ziggy no longer expected hedges in the fields. The hawthorn came out. Theodora wrote them asking them to dig her garden. Sue and Alex visited. Jake made friends with the taciturn barn-tenant and helped him with his chores. They were very happy.

Ziggy looked at the flat fields around him, the green stripes of sprouting furrows, the quarried river valleys and thought, it's like England, but stretched. Then shuddered as he thought of winter here — wind bellowing across the frozen fields, mice and loneliness in the night. He lit the oil lamps instead of the electricity and read Jake Wordsworth from Theodora's old school anthologies.

Summer school was coming. Theodora reclaimed her house. Jake had to go to camp. Ziggy wondered how he would react, but at the bus station in Toronto Jake saw his mother with his trunk, his camp friends leaping in excitement, and sprinted yelling into his other life. Ziggy felt the city burgeoning around him. He rolled his shirt-sleeves past his black fly bites, told Rosebud he had another engagement for lunch and went to prowl among the lunching girls at City Hall.

MARSHALLENE ON RAPE

1. I have never been raped. I have never raped anyone. My conscience on the matter is therefore almost clear.

2. There are however spring days in this fortieth ripe year when as the breeze comes in even this bedroom window (laden with gas fumes and noisy with motorcycles) when the idea seems less than impossible. If one were male . . .

3. Rape is a very old word. The *Compact Oxford Dictionary* Guy gave me for Christmas defines rape as the act of carrying off anything by force, particularly a woman, particularly violating her. It goes back to the Latin, *rapere,* which goes back to Mucius Scaevola thrusting his hand in the burning brassiere.

4. You can also say "in a rape" for in a hurry, or buy a rasp called a rape. A rape is a shire-division of England, or a kind of turnip, the common one; or charlock, or field mustard.

5. The only rapist I have ever known was my brother Byron, who at the age of fourteen fell on a girl named Shirley Lime in a ditch, and when she resisted, strangled her. I was only four at the time, but the event reverberated through our family. He was put away for life (I think they let him out once and he did something awful again, but I am not in touch with anyone who will tell me what) and now is only renowned for poems in the penitentiary magazine. Judging from the imagery (black swans in heat, etc.) I would not let him out.

My sister Mona was his only defender. She said he had taken her lots of times in the attic. She said all the kids did it. She

105

said Shirley Lime was stuck-up. My father repaid her loyalty with many strokes of his belt. Later, she ran away with a rather giggly Indian boy named Charlie. She now leads a sensible life on the reserve, where sex is not so often a cause of murder as it is among us. I picture her waking early among reedy islands to the call of water birds.

6. Rapees I have known:

I suppose "rapeable" was really what F. Tennyson Jesse meant when she wrote that essay dividing girls into "trunkable" and not trunkable. I in my young years was definitely trunkable but I managed to avoid the worst by colluding frequently in what was then considered — the worst. Wanda, who was, she claims, raped while babysitting, wore similar transparent postwar nylon blouses, spit curls, uplift bombardier brassieres and scarlet lipstick. The busdriver who allegedly did the deed claimed she incited him. The judge was not any more sympathetic to Wanda than the community was.

Anne, on the other hand, was raped at University and by a careless man who left behind the same fingerprints as were left in another groundfloor rapee's dormitory window. She was treated with such sympathy that the police helped her find a good abortionist. She said later it wasn't as bad an experience as the one she had last year when she had been left in the lurch by a jesuitical Ph.D. candidate.

Michelle, my ex-babysitter, after working a year in a Toronto rape-clinic, hitchhiked to the west full of confidence. She did all right with other hitchhikers, professors, truck drivers, salesmen and loggers, but in the depth of the bush a Rotarian in a grey car, wearing a grey suit, got the better of her. Young and wise, knowing the Puritan conscience, she lay back, but did not enjoy it. He drove her to the nearest bus station (she was afraid he would leave her on the forest road) after she promised not to tell the police. She told him to see a shrink, and me that the police would have laid a bad trip on her for hitchhiking. She is not what I'd call sexy, but somebody's sexy to everyone. Now, she washes her hands a lot.

7. How to avoid rape: NEVER GO OUT ALONE AT NIGHT: Aunt Hilda, to whom I owe a debt of gratitude for putting me

through highschool. ALWAYS WEAR RUNNING SHOES WHEN YOU GO OUT ALONE AT NIGHT: Johanna Frobe, to whom I owe a debt of gratitude for letting me get through university without attracting any men. The real loneliness of the long-distance runner.

8. The greatest rape scene in literature: In *And Quiet Flows the Don,* where the milk-maid type flaunts her bust around the place where the regiment is quartered and they finally go and take her, one by one, leaving her twitching like a frog in the hay at the end. Great stuff for fantasies. The literature of rape is incomplete from the female point of view, so that how rape affected the brain before 1970 is pretty well unknown. I notice the gap is now being filled in feminist papers.

9. EXCRUCIATING CONVERSATIONS I HAVE HEARD: Ken Morden at lunch today, discussing what he would do to any man who raped his daughter. The variations on the theme were distasteful. If I were Morden's beauteous daughter, I would leave home. He was eating salad as he talked: crunch, crunch.

Afterwards, I went to the Jewish Y and stood in the showers and scrubbed. In the pool, I ran into Ziggy Taler, who has also put on weight. I had not realised how well-made he was, however short. He has marvellous concentrated legs, now bowed. I had also not noticed that we have both aged considerably. We pretend to be twenty, hale-fellow-well-met, and we are not. We went for a beer and then to his place. After living with Guy for six months, I needed Ziggy. Also, it is spring, the wind is in the willows. Thank God, Ziggy is vulgar. I feel a traitor to Women's Lib when I am with him, he has a sexist attitude towards women, which is why his face is longer and sadder, why his marriages are always breaking up. It's probably a fatal flaw in his psychological nature, a failure to be able to sustain a relationship, etc. But in the sack, he isn't a gentleman. And what good is a gentleman in the sack? He likes sex, a rare quality in gentlemen over forty I meet these days. Genuine appetite must never be run down. I'm sorry it hasn't done him any good.

He likes sex and he likes big women (though I think he thinks it's nicer to be married to little ones, more fool he) and since I have not got smaller since I was Miss Sombrero Township in 1952, I do not feel when I am with Ziggy that I have quite gone out of style; more like a manuscript that's found a publisher.

He was on at me to describe the other women in the shower room; fancy that in anyone who's read *Portnoy*. I had to fantasize a little for him, they've all shrunk away. When we were at school we all had big legs like Percheron horses, and pony tails, and Rose Marx brassieres with strings six feet long we pulled tighter than Scarlett O'Hara's corsets for each other. The flat-chested ones went home and cried themselves to sleep. Anyone under fifty except me at the Y is skinny as a rake. Guy keeps telling me I'd better do something about it.

I haven't laughed so much for years as I have with Ziggy. He didn't start out much either, though there was a bias in favour of education in his parents where mine had given up. Still, the aunts and uncles helped us and we got off that farm my father wasn't interested in farming.

I haven't had such a good time for so, so long.

10. Causes of Rape: If your old man beats you with a razor strop, why not rape someone? Is that it?

No, there's more to it and I haven't read the right books. I would think from what I've heard, though, that Byron was an untreated hyperactive kid. They describe him as "seething" and "always being at" things. I remember him a bit. He was small for his age and he used to put his hand up my dress. But there were so many of us, and the Depression was on. My parents didn't know what to do with children, they just had them and tried to beat them into shape. Ridiculous to suggest that Ma could have loved us more. She was small, she had the three boys, then the girl who died, then Mona, who was cross-eyed, then the rest of us. The only one she loved was the girl who died, and maybe Len, the oldest.

Oh, the hell with going back to all that. Aunt Hilda says that of all the girls, mother was the only one who never just naturally instinctively picked up a baby when one was around. I guess she liked sex, she was healthy, then when everything went all to hell in the Depression they had nothing but 50 bad acres to fall back on.

11. Got home late and I guess I didn't make a sound on the stairs. When I opened the door I heard Roby, my Roby, saying "Oh, no, don't . . .!" in his changing, squawking voice. And I rushed in and

there was Guy holding him down on the bed, wrestling I suppose, but Roby knows a hawk from a handsaw.

"Get out," I screamed, "get out you frigging Rosedale bastard. Get out you fairy godmother, fellationist, neurophysiological failure."

Not as good as Captain Haddock, but it seemed to do. Guy, the elegant, stood up, red in the face and said coolly, "Hell hath no fury like a woman scorned."

They had their clothes on. Maybe he was just pinning his shoulder back.

Roby stood up. He's thirteen and getting glorious. I remember his father wasn't ugly. He has blue eyes in a good Irish blazing way, and he's tall, his body's pulling itself together. He turned to Guy, "You heard what my mother said, get out."

Guy sat down on the edge of the bed and began to shake.

We went into the kitchen. Roby put the kettle on. Then he said, "I'm glad you're not going to marry him."

"Mercy, no," I said, in my Aunt Hilda's voice.

Roby made the tea with the kind of masculine care I always respect. No just slopping the bags in the saucer. We sat for a long time, listening to Guy drag out suitcases and hunt in the closets for boxes. "Well," I said, "it appears you've grown up. Does he do that often?"

Roby shrugged. "He's been kinda, after me. But only in a way."

"He should see someone."

"Do shrinks really help?"

"They can show the right hand what the left has been doing."

But there's no church in Roby so I had to explain. He took it seriously and stood up in a grown-up sort of way and went down the hall to talk to Guy.

As he left the room I had such a surge of longing I couldn't remember the day I locked eyes with Guy and kidnapped him home — a big, loose-limbed, etiolated — well, gentleman. I thought of poor old Morden and his daughter.

Guy appeared. White. My generation. Not knowing what to say. He leaned on the doorpost. Upper Canada College didn't

teach him that. He looked like a clever bunch of bleached aspar-
agus. "Something else would have happened," I said to him, "but
I don't think you should muck about with kids. They don't know
how sexy they are."

"I'm sorry," he said hoarsely.

"You better go and see someone."

"I guess I will."

"I'm the wrong person for you. You don't really like the way
I live. You diverged because of that, but still . . ."

"Sure, Marsh."

"Godspeed, then."

Roby helped him down to the car with his grips, not looking
at all like a kid.

12. I don't think people who haven't been raped should write
about rape; on the other hand, who will? We must make out with
what we can find, we must make do, make ends meet, compromise
and do unto others as we would have them do unto us.

CHILDREN
AND
ANCESTORS

MEREDITH AND THE LOUSY
LATIN LOVER

MEREDITH came in early. Her mother was on the phone, talking as if there were trouble, but the living room door was closed, so she couldn't hear the words. She went up to her room as quietly as she could. She wanted a little peace. She had been over at Nicola Andrews' whose mother had bought the wrong kind of olives for the martinis, whose father was therefore shouting at her. Nicola went into a kind of crazy trance when her parents fought. They couldn't work on the project together, so Meredith had just put on her coat and come home. Some people's parents, she thought, are a dead loss. She thanked her lucky stars she and her mother lived alone and got on well together.

Up in her room, she found a bunch of new-old clothes on her bed. Her mother didn't need to shop at the Sally Ann any more but she couldn't give it up. She bought crazy armloads of things, and they fixed some of them up and shoved the rest in the Crippled Civilians box on the corner. Fun.

She took off her jeans and her tee shirt and looked at herself in the mirror. She was a funny shape, as lean, her mother said, as a fish. Her breasts were small, she had no belly and no hips, and she ate like mad, though never potatoes. Her mother was all bulges and curves like a Gibson Girl. They couldn't either of them figure out how women had changed so much. She guessed it was the diet, because everybody in her mothers' old school yearbooks looked like Gibson Girls; well, not as good as that, really. Lumpy, with funny long skirts and bobby socks and little teeny curls on their head. Awful. She thought her mother was much improved, though her arms were kind of punky.

She went through the clothes. Two awful sweaters. Mother, really, you should have saved your quarters. Then a funky maroon rayon dress with little flowers and a peplum. It looked like the real thing from the 'forties, but it probably wasn't. It would go with platform sandals.

She strutted and turned. Smoothed the peplum over her hips. Decided she looked sexy. If she wore it to school, they would all just die. She always wore jeans. They'd accuse her of being in drag.

She went downstairs. "Hey, Mum!"

Her mother opened the living room door. Her eyes were red. "Thought you were staying at Nicola's."

"I can't stand it when her mother and father have a fight."

"Don't blame you. The dress looks cute. I thought it would fit. It's a bit long, that's all. Got it for a dollar."

"I was wondering where I'd wear a thing like this."

"I wondered that too, but it seemed so you I bought it anywhere. Hang it up and you'll get a chance.

"Cleaners first, I think."

"Rayon stinks, doesn't it? Listen, I have to talk to you."

She looked at her mother carefully. A big woman with coils of strong black hair like snakes. She was so strong; but good-tempered. She was wearing black pants and a sweater and a scarf around her neck, as if she was dressed up to go out, but she looked terrible. Bad news. "What's happened?"

"Something really embarrassing. I don't know how to break it to you."

"Maybe I should make you a martini. I know how, now. That's what the Andrews were fighting about."

"I wouldn't mind if you got me a beer. I'm exhausted."

Which was not the usual tack her mother took, so Meredith went to the kitchen. My mother's funny, she thought. She says she drinks beer because it's democratic. I think she likes it because it's fattening. She's crazy, but the right way. She looks like a gypsy. How can Nicola stand her folks? I guess you have to.

Back in the living room she found her mother curled up on the chesterfield chewing her fingernails. It must be bad.

"Here, Nancy."

"Thanks, kid."

"So what's the news? You look the way you did when you lost your job at Civil Liberties."

"And I didn't know I'd get a better one. I should have had faith. Well, maybe this gig will turn out okay too, but I hate it."

"Hate what?"

"Your father's back."

To her amazement, Meredith started to cry.

Nancy held her a long time. "It's going to be okay, baby. It's okay. It was a shock to me too."

They had lived happily together for fifteen years, every since the day the Lousy Latin Lover walked out with the Swedish job and Nancy discovered herself as Sole Tenant, and found she was glad. Do this, do that, he had said, be this, be that. Never, be yourself and do the necessary and then what you want, and I'll help you. "I thought he was the cat's pyjamas," she told Meredith. "The bee's knees. The sun and the moon. He was tall and dark and handsome, all those legendary things. He was a good necker, I admit that, but once we'd had our white wedding I found myself under orders to do all the things his Mum had done, and she was a very passive lady, which I am not. When I was pregnant with you I found out about the Swedish bod. He told me he couldn't do without sex so I pretended I understood — I was staining and the doctor said we shouldn't. But when you were about two and he was still seeing the Swedish bod, I'd had enough. He walked out. Got a job in California, teaching at Berkeley. Fine with me. I wouldn't have wanted to go there. Three-quarters of a continent between us. Super. And you were all mine. I got the house and ten dollars a week support and thought I was in clover."

Now she was saying. "I don't know what to do, I don't know what to do," and biting her fingernails. Much worse than when she lost her job.

Meredith was used to feeling with her mother, taking on her moods and attitudes; but this time she also had a strange surge of hope which grew stronger as her mother worried on about her father's male-chauvinist-piggery, his machismo, his insensitivity, his fundamental blind decency. I have a father, she thought. Even though I haven't heard from him all my life, I have a father. The thought felt good.

But she was Nancy's child, not his. Nancy had done all the work, all the loving. She loved Nancy, she knew it. She wasn't able like the other girls to go around swearing about her mother. So she suppressed her hope and said, "What does he want, Mum?"

"He wants to take you out to lunch," Nancy said, and started bawling.

The next day when she got home after four she found the puppy chewing a letter for her. It was a formal note, slid through the letter box by hand, asking her to meet her father at a restaurant near Bloor Street on Saturday.

She felt torn, very torn. She knew she would go. She knew her mother would hate it if she went, and ask her questions and begrudge. This morning Nancy had been black, pure black. She had never seen Nancy black. She hated it.

At supper, she said defiantly. "He's asked me to lunch, and I'm going, Nancy."

Nancy looked at her quietly. "I think you're right."

"But you hate it."

"The mere thought of him drives me up the wall. The thought of you with him — jeepers. But he's your father."

"I don't know if I'll know him."

"Take a look at the wedding picture again. He probably has white hair. His father went white early, he told me. But the nose and chin will be the same. Wear the maroon dress. It'll look good on you; but if you buy platform sandals I'll strangle you. They're so tarty."

Saturday Nancy went down to the market and stayed out while Meredith strutted and primped and tried on attitudes. "Daddy," she said to herself, with an American nasal A, like the kids on the Brady Bunch. "Father . . . Fatha . . ." yes: a Forsyte Saga accent was better. What the hell was his first name? Edmondo. A crazy name. Though as her mother had explained he was not your ordinary Italian immigrant, or he'd never have got a visa to the States. He was a physicist, and a good one.

Daddy. Papa. Faaaa-ther. Pere. Pater.

She didn't feel as if she was going to meet her father at Noodles. She felt as if she were going to meet a glamorous older man.

She took off the maroon dress and put on her jeans, a clean tee shirt, and cork-soled clogs.

They had no trouble recognising each other. His hair was white here and there, but he was the same person as in the wedding picture: marvellously sleek and handsome. "Meredith," he said. She caught herself swooning. There were tears in his eyes. They moved towards the table in a dumb, vague mist, and their hands shook when they read the menu.

The conversation was not romantic. "I'm sorry I haven't been in touch. Your mother seemed to want you all to herself."

"We've had a super time together. She's really cool. I can't see why you left her."

"I felt she wanted me to."

"She said she loved you but you used to screw around."

He winced. "She's a very possessive woman."

"I guess you had all the freedom and she had none."

"Tell me what you're doing in school. Women's Studies and what else?"

They came by the end of the lunch, to a sort of arrangement. They would lunch again. He would bring his wife. She would call him Edmondo. They would not discuss her mother.

Nancy, haggard, was at the window. "How was it?" popped out faster than she apparently wanted to because then she went off on a tangent about the market, and it was a long time before Meredith could tell.

After she told, Nancy sat silent awhile, then said, "It's a wise child who knows its own father."

"I think I have to, Mum."

"You have every right."

"Don't get uptight about it, eh?"

But she did get uptight; she seemed to get paler and paler. Saturdays became a nightmare. All the words were encased in silences that had never happened before.

MEREDITH AND THE LOUSY LATIN LOVER

Meredith liked her father. Not his attitude to women, but his own self. He was clever and knowing and not like anyone else she knew. He made easy, affectionate conversation. He had been everywhere, seen everything. So many of her mother's friends were involved in local politics to the exclusion of anything else. He made them seem provincial. He made her boyfriend seem the age he really was. He made her mother seem unreasonable.

She liked his wife, too; she was not Swedish. Rather, a paint-smart Californian who taught at the Islamic Institute, and knew about a lot of fascinating things like Mohammedan theology. She called Meredith Merry. They always had a good time together. As the year progressed they began to invite her to their apartment which was on the 28th floor of a highrise and flooded with light. Meredith felt like a different person, raised above the darkness of downtown Victorian houses and civic idealism.

Guiltily, she watched Nancy go into a kind of decline. She got greyer and fatter and thin about the mouth. She heard herself shouting at her mother, "I have a right to see him once a week if I want. Your vibes are so bad. You're jealous. You always taught me it was stupid to be jealous. You're a hypocrite."

"Go and live with them, then," her mother said. "If you feel like that, just go and live with them. I'm not good enough for you, you're slumming . . . but let me tell you that lousy Latin lovers never did anyone any good."

After that one, she didn't know if she was alive or she was dead. It was May. She walked out of the house and stormed around town in a fit, crying. Once, she bumped into a cement telephone pole and chipped her front tooth. By the time it was dark she found herself on University Avenue. She crossed to the middle and marched down the parks of the boulevard, kicking tulips. There were no cops around to stop her. She took off her shoes and walked through all the fountains.

Finally, she found a dime in her jeans and phoned them. He was out, but Aviva, his wife was there and said to come right away, she'd be in the lobby with money for the taxi.

They sat in the great light room with the lights dimmed. Aviva put Vivaldi on the stereo, the Four Seasons. She gave her a glass of brandy to warm her up, even if it was against the law.

It was a beautiful experience, high up in the dark. They sat and mourned her mother. "I'm so terribly sorry," Aviva said. "This is the first time she's been unreasonable about anything and she's being totally unreasonable. It must hurt you very much. She's acting like a child, isn't she, or a puppy. She's so afraid he'll take you away from her that she wants to give you away before that happens. You mustn't let her, Merry. She doesn't really want to. And Edmondo was very young when they married. So was she of course. She didn't know how to manage him."

Edmondo came in quietly like a shadow and turned on her a look of grave, dark-eyed, concern. She started to cry. He went to reach out to her but Aviva shook her head. "Go to Nancy," she said. "I will keep Meredith to-night, but never again except for a holiday when she runs away from her husband. Go to Nancy. Give her back her girl, Edmondo. You are wicked never to have been to see her since you came back to Toronto."

In the morning, the apartment looked curiously uptight to Meredith. It seemed too neat, too mechanical. Though she had never slept on such sheets.

Edmondo was subdued at the breakfast table. Meredith didn't utter two words. Aviva buzzed around with coffee pots and apologised for their not having any milk. Finally Edmondo said, "I think she needs you, Meredith."

"Okay." Trying to think of home and almost failing.

Aviva said, "We are leaving for Russia in ten days. We'll be too busy packing to have lunch on Saturday. Anyway, it's better. She and Edmondo have had it out. The air is cleared. When we get back, everything will be different."

She was a good girl. She did as she was told. But instead of taking the subway she walked the whole way, thinking how different the city looked at night and in the morning. Thinking, I don't want anyone to own me, I won't let them have the papers. And, oh Jesus, I forgot to ask him about the math problem.

Nancy was asleep when she got home. She let her lie. Took a shower. Pranced in front of the mirror again. Something about her body was different.

She lay on her bed and thought about the Lousy Latin Lover. He was gorgeous, the sight of him made her quiver, but he couldn't do anything without Aviva. He was afraid of her a little, too. He always hesitated before he spoke. It seemed to her he didn't know how to be a father. His own father had been killed in one of their wars, and his mother was a martinet in black, Nancy said. She guessed he had his problems.

Well, I've got mine, she thought. Math. French. I wish he'd shell out so I could go to French Summer School. Nancy hasn't got the bread. If I have to work in the snack bar again I'll go out of my mind. She said she'd pay for a course but not out of town. I'd really get off on working for Dr Morris at the Museum. Shelley said he's cool, maybe he'd give me a job if I went and asked him.

When she heard Nancy get up she went down and made some coffee for her. They sat together, but they did not speak of the Lousy Latin Lover.

Nancy thought, I'm glad they don't have weddings any more. I won't have to worry about whether to invite him or not.

Meredith thought, I don't want to get into it with her. There are some things she just doesn't know. She's never been to Noodles in her life. I'm young and she's old. I'm going to do a lot of things. I'm going to leave her behind. Before, I didn't know how I could do that.

ONLY GOD, MY DEAR

S HE was invigilating a Latin exam, her mind, trapped as
usual (because it was three o'clock in the afternoon),
between plans for supper and plans for tomorrow. She felt
lighthearted when she remembered that the makings for supper
were at hand, that tomorrow's work involved only supervision as
well.

She taught English. The group today were her home form.
At one-thirty, when they began, she had handed around foolscap
and examination papers and had been conscious as she always was
during exams that she was not only herself but also her father.
When she began to teach, that frightened her, the way in which
she was not only herself when she stood before a class in certain
stances, but also her father, a combination of throwback and imitation. She got over the fear eventually, and now took pleasure in
the duplication of certain acts and attitudes. He had been a good
teacher, not a tyrannous one. His image was permanently with her
as a form of self-consciousness and complicated her teaching: she
was not only handling a class and a subject, but watching two
oddly-assorted personalities in herself. It was like being in a play
and seeing your beau and your parents and two critics in the front
row, going through the part reasonably well but never taking flight
because your inner eye was fixed on them.

She had returned to teaching four years ago, when Lisa was
twelve and Scott fourteen. She found it pleasantly easier, for
raising the children had developed some dignity, some authority,

that she had only latently before possessed. Last week she had heard two of the girls snickering about "Old Walpole's rat coat" and looked down almost with wonder to see that her fur coat, that had been a graduation present from her parents, was indeed a desiccated collection of dead muskrat. She laughed with them. Part of the fun of teaching was verbal cut-and-thrust. To be "Old Walpole" was to be both permanent and involved.

Thirty of them in her home form, hunched over inky fingers. She was fond of them now, the September strangeness was gone off them. Some of them were her children's friends. They were tall and alive and athletic — even her own children had these ridiculously prolonged legs — unbent, unaccustomed to uniform. And enormously hairy. And just as vulnerable.

They scorned her for thinking them babies, but to her they seemed immensely young: their faces were bland and unlined, strained with uncompromising hope. They were the same mixed bag you always got in a form: A. with problems because of a broken home, B. with acne and acute self-consciousness, C. a compulsive show-off, D. suffering from undiagnosed horrors, E. and F. and some of the others "normal" and what is called popular and working below the level of their intelligence, and setting the style for the school. A few of them were talented, two of them were brilliant. The majority coasted.

This annoyed her. She could not, without dragging them over her shoulders on a sledge, bring them up to any sensible level of literacy. Achievement was unfashionable, the great Guru McLuhan said books were going out. In spite of this she snapped at their heels and chivied them, and fought committees that plugged the curriculum with senselessly easy books. Although, on the whole, she had had enough of fighting. One has only so much character to assert, one can mend only so many socks and so many comma splices. It would not do to be ridiculously self-sacrificing: one's self was split into too many parts: home, school, family, and the private, neglected life of the imagination.

But since the life of the imagination came to her through words, and words were important to her there was in the school a certain respect for, and a certain fear of Old Walpole.

There were things she could not and would not abide: bad

grammar from those who taught, punctuation in dots and dashes (Who do you think you are, Queen Victoria? she asked them furiously). Bad, expensive text-books (she had once hurled one out an open window yelling, "Graft!"), waste and the girls' long hair.

It looked, she thought, better than the crimped hair they had worn in their day. But it got into their eyes and their mouths, it hung down and blotted the papers of the few who still used ink. They chewed it noisily and obscenely, they skewed their forelocks into little Chassidic ringlets all ignorant of the tradition, they dangled it over three desks at a time. They had yards and yards of it, they spent their evenings under portable driers and not reading, they pressed it and coloured it, and each year that the hair got longer, the work got worse. It was, she thought, an insult to the intelligence.

The boys' she did not mind: few of them grew it long enough to get in their way, and since they had started to grow it, they had developed a lurid and individualistic beauty reminiscent of Victorian religious engravings; one saw their bleeding hearts outside their shirts, and a row of hoarse-voiced pubescent students was no longer a row of incipient Rotarians and football players. But the girls; it was women's hair she loathed, that was a kink in her. She had kept her daughter's short until she was old enough to have braids, and made war on hair in the sink and the bath-drain, and hairbrushes clotted with snarls and lying on the chesterfield: it spoke to her of misty female horrors, far-off invalid aunts and lyings-in: she was very strict on the matter to her daughter Lisa, who laughed at her.

No doubt the fashion would change, but the fact remained, they could not see with that hair and the work showed it. Therefore, after the bice-lined foolscap, after the examination paper, she passed out elastic bands. And the ones she had known for the whole four years, who knew her and knew she liked them, and liked her when they did not hate her, accepted the elastics, and tied back their flowing locks, and worked. The others, eternally puzzled, "The Soul's Awakening" rising from the inkwell, eternally pushed with their fingers the spider-webs from their faces. She thought again, how very like my father.

As they wrote, she marked a few second-form papers. Not

many: there was not much concentration. There were the aisles to heel against cheating, the hands raised for foolscap. One of the girls went yellow, she opened the window. They scribbled and sighed.

The atmosphere was cool and yet heated: one of the tense beauties of the examination season. The good ones came in, trained like runners, and applied themselves to the challenge. The socialites were laggard. She felt sorry for the ones who were afraid, who failed to understand the joy of walking the tightrope between control and aberration. The electricity of hypertension in the air, the earnest quietude, and the kind of pen they used no longer scratched. She watched them half enviously. This was what people meant who said that school days were the best days of their lives, that the children would never again experience anything as simple and finite in its excitement as examinations, except, perhaps, later, the pleasures of the chase, and within its framework the experience was superb.

More and more of them, of course, were coming to believe that the framework was wrong. She suspended judgment.

She rose very quietly to announce that examination time was over, and trod on the balls of her feet as her father had (he was a soothing presence in an examination hall) while she collected the papers. It reminded her of the time-signal in England: you dialed a certain number in London and a slow, modulated, infinitely soothing voice enunciated: The time/is now/three/twenty/nine.

They left the classroom drained and exhausted. A few were grumbling, a few were faint with competition. The Ablative Absolute was never easy and these kids fought logic harder than previous generations. She found it interesting that Hal Chambers had reverted to the old three-cycle scarlet Caesar they had used in her day. He was a good teacher. They wrote better English because of his Latin.

Kyra Clarke returned her elastic with a grin and a bob. "Thank you, Mrs. Walpole."

When she got home, she put her brief-case down and donned a kind of mental armour. Shoved the cat out the door, sped upstairs to make sure the beds were made. Went to the bathroom, picked up the men's sluttish underwear from the floor, dashed down with the laundry hamper. Put the oven on pre-heat and did the washing. Then she peeled carrots — they were all, thank God, crazy about carrots — threw canned tomatoes and kidney beans and chili powder in yesterday's extra spaghetti sauce. To-morrow she would do better, with the afternoon off, she would cook something that needed watching. Scott thundered in and headed for the breadbox. "Where's Lisa, Scotty?"

"Women's Lib."

"Good God, at exam time? How was chemistry?"

"Breeze. Been playing hockey."

"What have you got tomorrow?"

"Trig and physics. Need oxygen for that. Got 'em taped, though."

"Half a loaf, half a loaf, half a loaf onward. Supper at six."

"Yeah. Listen, Ma, I think I flunked English."

She stopped her domestic flutter and turned to face him. He was looking at her tentatively. "It's your English, not mine," she said. "Flunk it if you want, you yob." The school was big enough so that he would never be in her class.

"I can't write all those crummy essays," he said. Again she refused the challenge. "I'm going to mark some papers," she said. She worked at the kitchen table.

"Yeah, sure." He was having an endearing stage of pretending to be insensitive, which went with a less endearing stage of condescending to her. She thought, he should be off and away this year, the school system runs too long.

"Maybe you could ask Mr. Potter if I did all right," he added.

"Maybe you could grate the carrots."

"Sure. I thought you were going to boil them."

"Not if you're around."

"OK, I'll do it."

"Thanks."

"I gave out elastics this afternoon," she said. "I really can't take all those English sheepdogs."

"Yeah, Kyra told me. They think you're a character."

"She can write."

"Poetry?"

"I haven't seen any. Sentences, I meant. That's where it's at, you know."

"I've heard the commercial." He crunched on the grater. She liked his fearlessness. She had been carefully brought up to fear sharp instruments and when she made *carotte rapée* she translated it as cuticle salad.

Ted was next home, laughing. "Know what?" Lisa's outside the Royal York picketing a bathing-beauty contest."

"At this time of year?"

Scotty snorted. "They've got to her."

She began to defend her daughter. "It *is* humiliating . . ." But she could think of no way of going on without offending their ears, for the only way to make them understand was to adopt a male vocabulary which hurt their feelings. And there was the business of getting at the exam papers. She left them and went back to the kitchen.

When the phone rang, Ted took the call. Afterwards he came in and said, "That was Lina."

"Goodness, what does she want."

"She wants me to come over to-night; some trouble with the lease. You're marking to-night, aren't you?"

They had always known Lina, and always quarrelled over her. She had not married, and she had once been very beautiful, although her present appearance was open to argument. It could not be said that Lina because she was beautiful had failed to use her head; it seemed to Diana that she used it admirably. Certainly she told good stories, and they sounded wonderful to other women's husbands.

"Don't go, Ted. She'll only get you involved again."

"Why not? You're busy."

"So I am." She let the jealousy show in her voice, and knew that Ted would go.

At the dinner table, poetry crept in among the shredded carrots. Lisa was radiant.

"Keeping down the white slave trade, are you?" her father teased.

She bounced with fury. Diana and Scotty thumped their spoons and shouted, "Unfair, unfair."

Lisa when her colour was high might have won a beauty contest herself, praise the carrot. Now she was all angry vitality. "Daddy, you can't imagine what they do to them, parading them like cattle, ugly old broadcasters kissing them . . ."

"They want to be paraded like cattle and kissed by old men," Ted said. "They want to win the prize, the ticket to Hollywood, the flashy car. They want to hear hands clapping."

"I think it's horrible," Lisa said, near tears now.

"Oh come on, Lise, where's your sense of humour? Anyway that's all going out, now."

"Not fast enough for me."

Diana broke in. "Do you know the Yeats? 'That only God, my dear/Could love you for yourself alone/And not your yellow hair'?"

"Mother, if that's what literature is for I can't see why you teach it."

Diana thought suddenly, I never liked that verse either. She said to Lisa, "I'm glad you believe in what you're doing."

Ted snorted. "She'll be blowing up radio stations next."

Lisa gave him a look that stated that her personal bombs would be dedicated to law offices.

"Mum gave out elastic bands to-day," Scotty said.

There was a cross-generational complicity of looks before they left the table. They went upstairs to study.

She cleared the table and thought how easy it was to be unfair to Ted. His teasing was always a probe and sometimes an insult, but in fact he saw the world steadily and whole and not in subjects as she did. It was he who had kept the children, too, from rebelling against her scholasticism. If, deep inside, there was an old fuddy-duddy who salivated at beauty contests, should she complain?

But after he went to Lina's, she was distracted, unhappy. It was stupid to be jealous of Lina, and beneath her, and she was jealous of Lina. Lina was sinuous and capable, and men worked for her. "I don't have time for Ted to-night," she thought, "Why shouldn't he go there?" It was so very long ago that Lina was the

129

temptress and she was the ingenue. She went back to her papers.

After a point, however, the answers began to seem worse without being worse. She began to be pettish about punctuation. She laid the work aside, thought of the housework she might do and would not do, and turned on the television set in the middle of *David Copperfield.*

Steerforth. Good lord, Steerforth. David. Peggotty. Agnes. Dora. Barkis is willin'. And the way Mother said, "Dooora." My bedtime story. She told it better than the text, we cried: orphan children, to be covered with leaves. He was born with a caul, it meant he wouldn't drown. Steerforth. Emily, Dora, Agnes. Don't we know them: Dora with her hair in her eyes and that ghastly little dog.

She thought for a moment of calling the children down, and remembered they were children no longer. She could not envisage their sharing her reaction, and they had their own work to do. During a commercial, she called Lisa on the extension and told her to turn it on if she wanted to upstairs. Lisa said she was studying, and so was Scotty.

So she watched alone and cried unabashedly. If Ted were here he would be always conscious of the actors, the credits, the techniques. Well, it was her job to be conscious of the story and the voices, and they were lovely. Silly old Dora, Brave Agnes. Charles Lamb and dream Alice, Lear and the Stanley children and epilepsy. Ruskin and Carroll and little girls — to Yeats and the gold ramparts of yellow hair: what a century it had been. She cried, she cried. It was sentimental, gorgeous. Lost mums, lost friends, lost innocence, a childhood of funerals. Ham, the dog at their uncle's farm called Ham, faithful and lost for Steerforth.

Ted came in after the storm was over and she was waiting up with a drink. No need to be alert in the morning if there was no teaching, only presiding. She had heard the kids going to bed. "Well?" she asked.

He looked a little different, sheepish, embarrassed. She made a *moue,* he kissed it; she made him a drink, he took it. She let him marinate in the experience. He said, "She asked me to marry her."

"What?"

"That goddam silly bitch Lina had the gall to suggest that I leave you and the kids and marry her."

"Well I never!"

He sat back and undid his belt and his trouser top-button and whistled and grinned, stroking his memory ruefully. "I don't think I ought to tell you about it."

She was shocked — something in her stomach was beating a pulse — but somehow not surprised. "It must have been powerful," she said.

"It was."

She went out to the kitchen and put the kettle on. When she returned he was looking better. "I think I'd be flattered," she said.

"I suppose I was. All the same, Diana, she's got no decency at all."

"Well, I told you that."

The thing sat on them like a heavy dinner. "I'm sorry I've been so crass about her," she said.

"You were right, evidently."

"She used to come here when you were away and the children were small and I was constricted in my life, and tell me her troubles with her lovers."

"You used to go to her when she was feeling spinsterish and tell horror-stories of domesticity."

"Well, if she was thinking, Poor Ted, all along, she'd every reason to advance her proposition, hadn't she?"

"I suppose so."

"Do you want to go?"

There was a long pause and a small, "No."

"I don't see why anybody shouldn't be free if . . ." She stopped. That wasn't what she meant at all. She had had, as he spoke, a small shock of desire for freedom, the thought, only three of us, easier . . . "Goodness," she said. "What a time you've had."

"Remember the baby-sitter who used to say to you, 'You'll have to keep up with him and not lose your looks, Mrs. Walpole'."

"When I was fat after Lisa. You were so good, then. You held me together."

"What did you do to-night?"

"I watched *David Copperfield* on the television and cried and cried. I was darn glad you weren't here."

131

When they went upstairs both Scotty and Lisa were snoring powerfully. Lisa's light was still on, and Ted turned it out.

In their own room she asked, "Do you want me to give up work?"

"Don't ask big questions. I've had enough of them to-night."

She watched him undressing systematically: shoes, socks, cufflinks, sleeve garters (surely the last man in the world to wear them, and they always moved her), shirt. He had been shaken. Good on him. And poor for her if she deserved it.

"You'd better ease up on Lisa and women's lib," she said.

"You'd better ease up on the hair."

"Oh no, if I did that I wouldn't be myself."

"I wonder what Lina was after?"

"You."

"Oh, I suppose so. But there's always something more."

"I wonder if there's another way to live. Are you sure you don't want me to quit teaching?"

"You've got to use up all that energy somehow, haven't you? Good-night, love. I'm an old, old man tonight."

"Somebody ought to tell Lina a thing or two."

"Such as?"

"Well, there's nothing to marriage, is there? I mean, it's a transparent condition."

"Don't follow you."

"It's everything or nothing depending on how it develops, but not an object you grab."

"I guess not."

"David and Dora were marvellous."

"Were they?"

"She had this terrible little dog, a King Charles Spaniel or a pug, and she gave it mutton chops when there were none for them."

"Oh."

"He was a marvel, Dickens, wasn't he? In fact, the whole nineteenth . . ."

He put his hand firmly across her mouth. She meant to protest, but she fell asleep.

132

THE FALL OF THE HOUSE
THAT JACK BUILT

MARCUS was brooding again, standing in the bay window staring at the movers' trucks across the road. First he said, "The new President is from Georgia," giving the name an exaggerated southern accent, then he said, "I wonder if old Laidlaw built that mansion with an eye to selling it to successive captains of industry?" and then, "Do you think they'll change the initials on the awnings?"

Alissa was vacuuming. She could hear him, but she lacked the energy to shout in reply, or stoop to turn the machine off. The heat was stifling, and although the radio blamed the thick air on a temperature inversion, it was plain that now there were four mills in the town, one could no longer expect to breathe. It was July, the boys were off at camp. They had planned to spend the summer sailing and working on the house.

Marcus said, very loudly, so she could no longer pretend to be deaf, "There are four vans and a manager's panel truck. It's a *cara*van." She switched the machine off to show that she sympathised with the necessity to make bad jokes.

The dining room ceiling fell in.

They turned and stared blankly at it, as if a sheeted ghost had appeared to startle but not surprise them. There was a brief avalanche of plaster and then they were choking in plaster dust. Chunks that had fallen on the table looked like pieces of a jigsaw puzzle. "Wonder if the beam will hold?" he shouted to her. And although they were twenty feet from the catastrophe, he took on the look of a man who was in the middle of it; his tonsure ruffled and dusty, his clothes dishevelled, his eyes excited.

They were half glad, in fact, to see the ceiling come down. They had worked hard on the house, and the return to the home town. They had not been rewarded.

It had once been her grandmother's house. Both of them had scurried past its awesome towers on the way to public school. She had been frequently inside it as well, and been just as daunted by it: it was starched and crackling and rubbed the back of her neck like a new collar, and her grandmother was an unkind old woman who made sure she knew that dark-eyed left-handed children were a disgrace to the family, as opposed to her blue-eyed right-handed cousins, who were overpraised. When she grew up and married that dark foreign-looking Marcus who did well to become a teacher considering . . . she made peace with the old woman, who, astonishingly, left her the house.

The family pitied her. There were better pickings: certain stocks, certain sums of money banked at low interest for long time (the grandmother lived to be 94) and forgotten. The fair cousins said languidly, "We always knew she liked you better, but we'd rather have the Crown Derby and the Wedgewood." But Marcus was good with his hands and thought he would like to have the house to work on after the gruelling days at school, so they kept it.

It was not big for its day, but it was big for theirs and badly organised. The kitchen, for instance, was arranged for the persecution of immigrant slavies. There was an arrogant wood-burning furnace, meant to consume faggots bought cheap from the mill. The wiring was shocking.

They had slaved over it, convincing themselves that they were learning about building, about the history of building. For a while, Marcus talked animatedly about restoring the spirit of the house. They both took joy in ripping out bad modernisations installed by Alissa's bachelor uncle in the 'thirties, made of degenerate early versions of pressed wood. But after the first stage was finished, the wiring restored, the furnace converted, the upstairs insulated, the beaverboard rooted out and burned, it became clear that the house was in fact a monster, and that they were fools throwing good money after bad. For the foundations the place had were shifting, the frame siding itself was cracked, and when the engineers came to install the jacks in the basement that would hold the house up for another twenty years, they pointed out that the beams of the place were mill-seconds, and cracked. From that day Marcus went around the town glooming, "Second rate from the beginning."

The positive aspect of the experience was that it killed in Marcus certain feelings of inferiority he had suffered from since childhood. If the big McCreavy house was cracked, all of the big houses were cracked. That year, instead of working on the house, he bought the boat and joined the yacht club.

But they had gone on working on the house, obsessively decorating their nest with strings of coloured wool. Once the least practical aspects were dealt with, it was a good place to live in, and they liked the work.

So they stood beside the plaster, wondering what to do. "Goddammit," Marcus said. "Goddammit."

She thought irrelevantly, there was no wind to-day anyway.

They heard the beam crack. The house had shifted.

He sent her outside. She sat on the front step furthest from the overhang of the verandah while he phoned his engineer. Across the street, multitudes of movers were carrying furniture: ants shifting their eggs when you lift their sheltering cover. All the furniture was draped. She wondered where the people had lived before they lived in Georgia, where they bought their furniture. They would never get inside the house: the Mill did not mix with schoolmasters. Anyway, they wouldn't have belonged. Once when the president's wife was a lonely little person from Baton Rouge she had been invited over for gin beside the pool. She had begun by not knowing what to wear for gin beside the pool, and proceeded not to know what to say. She was from a different planet.

Her grandmother used to talk about Laidlaws, who built the house, and Hunters, who built the mill — not this one, but the first, or perhaps just the one that lasted — as if they were equals, human beings. That was before Hunters sold out to a big British outfit and took their profits to Toronto, before the other mills were built.

The movers wore striped aprons and were respectful of the

privet hedge.

Marcus came out to say that the crew would be around this afternoon. He was carrying a gin bottle. There was a dangerous gleam in his eye. They went around to the back of the house and drank gimlets in the ruins of the summerhouse.

For four nights in the hot soupy weather, they slept outside on top of their sleeping-bags, and wondered if the boys were having as good a time at camp. They were not overlooked. They made love. Once a raccoon came to watch. For only a couple of thousand dollars that they did not have, the jacks were adjusted, the beam across the house was replaced with a steel I-beam. "The wood culture is over," Marcus said, brandishing the gin he could not afford.

They moved inside, they removed the mess, they plastered the ceiling themselves and did a fair job of it, they complained about the heat and wrote letters about pollution and glared across the road at the servants of the people from Georgia. "It's not their fault, of course," Alissa said.

"Don't talk about fault, you'll make me think I'm back at school," he said savagely.

July was gone, suddenly. "We haven't sailed at all," she said.

"I'm going to sell that boat," he said.

"Oh no, Marcus. It's the only thing that makes you feel free."

"What're you going to do with the boys for August?"

"Let them stay home and run the streets. It's good for them. Summer's the time to get to know a place, and this year they're the right age to bicycle all over."

"And you?"

"I suppose I'll spend the month stripping the bannisters."

"The hell you will!"

He had reasons for his black moods, of course: but she was a little frightened by his growing savagery. "Well why not? It's been on the list for years."

"All you'll find under there is punky yellow oak. I'll paint them again for you."

"Well, what do you think we should do for the rest of the summer?"

"Take up Linda's invitation to the island. I'll stay here. I've courses to work on and there's a lot of thinking I want to do."

In the end, she did, and enjoyed herself. Linda was unfailingly good company, the children got on well together, she swam more than she had for years and came back brown and glowingly healthy to Marcus.

He led her into the house. "Don't panic. I'll explain." For a moment she expected corpses littered across the floor.

It was no longer their house; it was quite another house. It was a modernised interior from a decorating magazine, down to the tinkly front-hall chandelier. "Be careful of the rugs," he said. "They're only on loan."

"But it's *my* house, Marcus," she said, and started to cry. It was all slick and white-painted and there were nasty touches of gilt.

"I know, honey."

"What are you up to?"

"We can sell it now, Alissa."

"Well of all the . . ."

"I know. I know. What do you think of my paper-hanging?"

Nymphs and urns and cherubs stood on each others' heads all the way up the immense height of the stairwell. She started to laugh. "Wouldn't grandma have a fit? Who designed it?"

"I did. I got every goddam house and garden magazine and all the books out of the library."

"So we're going to sell it."

"It's your house."

"Not now, it isn't. Why didn't you cap it all with white broadloom?"

"Couldn't afford it. I rented the rugs from the Human Polar Bear."

The Armenian who went swimming on Boxing Day. "I guess you had to do something," she said. "Have you met the people across the road?"

"Did you think I papered that hall myself?"

"Really?"

"Yeah, he wandered in one hot night and said 'Hi there!' in a nice rich broth of a voice."

THE FALL OF THE HOUSE THAT JACK BUILT

"Ikons falling."

"Yeah. He doesn't know where we're at, but he's a good paper-hanger. He thinks we should ask seventy-five, now. Corner lot."

"Oh, Marcus."

"Well, if we can't win by playing our game, we have to play theirs, don't we?"

It was all so white and light that she did not know where she was in the morning. When she remembered what he had done she was troubled again, and mournful. Certainly Marcus was not a man to stand still, he had to keep acting. And it was ridiculous to be possessive about the house: without his work and his money it would have fallen long ago.

She had no idea what his plans were. If the man across thought they could get seventy-five, he was either going to help them sell to the Mill, from which they would get seventy-five, or he was thinking in American numbers. For seventy-five they could get a house further up the lake, and a cottage, and a second car and a better sailboat. Or they could go to some island. She winced when she thought of Marcus fomenting reconstruction on an island. She knew him better because of the boys, now: he always had to have something to do.

She agreed to the "For Sale" sign, she agreed to the sale. She showed the troups of ladies and gentlemen through. She lied to them about the heating bills. She pointed out the fact that the ripply glass in the bay window was original glass, without her usual witticism that 1897 was not a good year for glass. The Mill bought the house, and once the deeds were signed Marcus brought his lawyer along to straighten out the business about the money. The Mill paid cash. She put her half of the sum in a savings account for herself and the children. She would not buy mortgages with it. She wanted it available, for Marcus was looking restless.

Then they asked the people from across the road over for drinks. They slicked the boys' hair down with water, tidied themselves, and told Royce Beemer that no, they would not be happy if he dropped by tonight.

The Mill people called her "honey" and were charming. They refrained from talking politics, in fact gave the impression that they lived in a realm beyond politics. Mrs Delamere commented on the house. "You should have seen it before," Alissa said bitterly.

"It was your grandmother's house, wasn't it?" Mrs Delamere said in a voice that had a regretted, abandoned plantation behind it.

"Oh, I don't mind that," Alissa said, "it's just those wretched cupids . . ."

"Never mind, honey. They'll be going."

"Are there plans?" Alissa's hackles began rising. She looked over towards Marcus and thought, he looks well for the first time in years.

"Oh, I've heard an idea or two. Of course George — pardon me, I mean Marcus — was right to do it over in order to sell it, but I'd like to see one of these gorgeous old places restored . . ."

Alissa smiled grimly. She had known the house since she was born in 1936 and doubted if it had changed much in the previous forty years, except through the wanton and ham-fisted efforts of Uncle Eli. What they would restore would be an idea, and it would be hard to pin that down.

"What do you want to do now, Marcus?" Mr Delamere was asking.

Marcus looked blank, as if the idea that there was now something further to do was a surprise.

"Oh, go on teaching, I guess."

"Where're you going to live?"

"Oh, I guess we'll find a place."

"I saw a marvellous little yellow brick cottage for sale yesterday, just your thing, Marcus," Mrs Delamere said.

"I don't think we're in the restoration business any longer," Alissa said.

"Didn't your folks live here? You must know the town very well."

"Mum and Dad are in Florida, and Marcus's mother is dead. Maybe we'll push on to Toronto or someplace, if Marcus wants to."

Marcus had sunk into himself. "I dunno," he kept saying, "I dunno."

THE FALL OF THE HOUSE THAT JACK BUILT

The Delameres left early, and beamingly invited them to return the visit. They said they would.

In bed, she said, "Marcus, you're sick."

"Leave me alone."

"Not until we find another house, I won't."

"Women and their nests."

With part of her money, and part of Marcus's money, they bought a well-designed modern house on the lakeshore. They had their own beach, they paid their debts, the boys were rapturously happy. Marcus's colleagues muttered a little about inherited money, but were happy to come and swim there. For a while, Marcus took up drinking, then he bought a printing press and spoiled the look of the recreation room with it, which pleased her.

She walked on the beach a lot. One day in town, she met Mrs Delamere, who said she must take up their invitation and come over. She explained that she had not been to the old street, even to drive down it, that she did not want to go back to the old street. And she knew from Mrs Delamere's eyes that Mrs Delamere was living in that house, and that in front of it there would be a metal statue of a servant holding out his hand to receive the horses; and that to conform with the custom of the country Mrs Delamere, being a foreigner, would have purchased a white statue; whereas up on the lakeshore where they lived, the statues still had black enamelled faces.

MARSHALLENE AT WORK

TOSSIE in the raspberries, they said. Tossie in the raspberries.

And the oil and the debts.

Who'd have thought, they said, that Marshallene would grow up to write down the story of Tossie in the raspberries?

Who'd have thought, thought Marshallene, that they'd want to read about the raspberries? And do they have raspberries where the story started, in the place I called Frasertown for want of the name of it? And who'd have thought I'd write it down for them that way, and they'd like it, when I wanted to write it down a harder way, so they wouldn't like it? They're dying for a lick of themselves, whom before they scorned.

Tossie in the raspberries: a bone, all that was left. When they went to bury Uncle Herb, Walter and Byron (a story in himself, Byron, but one already told, a cliche . . . club-footed [did they know enough to name him for it?] and corrupt) dug into the plot beside Aunt Whatsername and down, down, until they found a bone, which didn't appeal to them. So they went over to Harcourt's to get the plan, and they traced it with their big-treaded forefingers, and it had been part of Tossie's brother, Big Allan, who, they didn't remember why, failed to survive. The first to die in the new land.

The land was not good. It bred lilac bushes, and a fine stand of beech they cut down first thing, though Tossie liked it, the one who was all feeling; but the land was not good. They had come

141

too late, taken land where the creeks ran black with tarry stuff and the mosquitoes were as big as butterflies, but the soil was stiff heavy clay that broke your heart and your plough. There was oil in the next township, but there was no oil all down their line. Some of them worked for the big oil men, James even went to South America and Bohemia, because there was oil, too, there and it was just beginning. The rest stayed on the land and borrowed to send one son each away.

So, as people will, dragging time behind them like tired ants, they made a history. Not much of a history — drought, disaster, occasionally distinction — James had made money and built a big house, Stanley was a professor, but something that was their own. And a little of it got told, and it was Marshallene who remembered.

How she heard, she did not remember. Someone told the stories, which of the old, old women was it, in black stockings and aprons over aprons, worn cardigans, men's slippers, white cataracted eyes? Somebody told somebody and it got down to Marshallene, maybe one of the days she went over to Lizzie's in case they had something to eat, and had an egg and a biscuit and a beating for it after, for begging.

When it was very bad, her mother used to say "We were good people," but Marshallene did not know until later, when her mother took her to live with the Macraes, what good people were. She thought she was good. She was better than Mona, who wasn't all there. She was better than Byron, who lost his temper and foamed at the mouth, and killed a dog with a stone. She was better than her mother, because when Walter beat her, she didn't whine.

All up and down the line, the land was theirs. They called the line the French line, because the first Heber had been French, not Heber but Hebert. But all he gave was his name and his red hair. Half of the family were feeble-eyed and red-headed from him: the rest were black Frasers and tarry-haired Macraes, big tough people, good people, except one in every generation, who drank or swore or borrowed or made pot liquor, like Walter in this one, who did them all.

When her mother gave up and took her and the twins to Mrs. Macrae, she was already twelve years old, she knew all the stories. She couldn't remember under what long oilclothed kitchen table she had heard them, but she knew them. Therefore she knew who she was.

She was particularly herself and after that, a descendant of that Tossie who had stood up against his mother in the raspberries and said, "I willna go to Canada unless you bring our Kate."

Tossie was that petted on Kate, they said. But Kate was in service at the Castle, not a housemaid, mind you, but almost a lady's companion to that forgotten lady's name. It was a step up, they told him. He couldn't take Kate from that. She was not his Kate: she was his sister, her own person.

Tossie went up to the castle and wept at the tower. Tossie pleaded. Kate shook her head. She hadn't but come, she was expected to stay. They sailed without her, ten of them altogether: John and Mary (they were all called John and Mary, those couples) and the eight of their children who could go, Kate being in service and Jorie feeble with the consumption at his Uncle's house.

That was all there was, really. Tossie was the one who had not cut down the trees. He lived to be an old, old man full of feelings and regrets, to marry a red-headed woman and to die owner of many trees. But first he worked like Jacob for his Kate, and bring her out, and leave two photographs of her in his tin savings box: one of a bright beauty with a high shell comb in her hair and ebony curls and a glister in her eye: and a haughty look. And another not taken much later of a broken-winged starling bedizened with limp silk flowers and starchless lace, and a button off: he had not done well.

Marshallene made a book of Kate and Tossie, and it was much liked. But it wasn't the book she wanted to make. She didn't know how to make it, or if it could be made. It would be made, she thought, with many blank pages, pressed flowers and rhymes like this:

In your wreath of remembering
Twine one bud for me.

Which is not a story, any more than Tossie defying his mother in the raspberry patch is story: but still it is.

And embossed stickers: a Greenaway girl on a stile; a speckled bird; a forgetmenot, a faithful dog.

MARSHALLENE AT WORK

Because there was an album of Kate's she had seen, and she had memorised the rhymes. "In thee," wrote the person who later founded the first advertising company in Toronto, "let joy with duty join/ And strength unite with love./ The eagle's pinions folding round/ the warm heart of the dove."

Lines written in a cold cabin on a stormy night?

What kind of life was it, really? She had made one up, and it had sold well. Though the Macraes hadn't appreciated it — she had had a strong letter from Mrs. Macrae, talking about letting the side down. Whose one aim in life was to prove to her daughter that she had nothing under her underpants, and that none of them ever came near the soil. No, that wasn't right, she was proud of the farm she came from. It was the idea of the earth that bothered her. She didn't need a book like *Lady Chatterly's Lover* to tell her how the world was. She'd got off the farm by wrapping her skirts tight around her legs and running; later, it became a way of life. The things that Marshallene must know were the things that worried her, and she made her promise not to tell those things to her Marjorie, who would have profited had she listened.

And that was a cool hundred years after the raspberry bushes. And Marshallene had beautiful white capped teeth to show there was profit in it: coming from somewhere, being. Telling the stories of it. Yet she wasn't satisfied. The common people, people as common, that is, as Hebers on the French line, do not make history: and yet they do. They drop their get like drops of dye in water, the image spreads. Faith dies, but the people live on in odd places, like Walter (whom she never called father), still living in that box of a house on the dismal plain, by the burned-down barn and the back kitchen the frost had heaved off its foundations, still living, now the government had inserted a heart-pacer and cured him of alcoholism. Walter waving his blackthorn stick at her and telling her she was no daughter of his now she'd married a Jew (her husband was an Italian, her first husband; her second had died, Osborne, whose name she used). Byron unrepentent in the Pen, writing black paranoid poems in the prison magazine (where did we get the words in us, she wondered. We weren't Irish enough to sing.) Len president of a chemical company: the one who made good. The mad twin a recognised philosopher, the sane one a housewife. Two dead in the war. The county crawling with scrawny cousins. And I said to Hal Osborne that's my uncle Jeb who operates that ferry and he said that what, and I showed him the scow you could inch across the river with your car on it: still cheaper than building bridges. And he didn't believe it. "It's the back of beyond," he said.

Marshallene sits and types and puts it all down one way, and Mrs. Macrae writes and says it's disgusting, babies were never made in the thickets in that country. And Marshallene looks at her work and wishes she knew another way to put it down, that was less gross and explicit, that would show like the secret life of Mona among the Indians (for she went to look for her and found that indeed she was on the Reserve, fat, middle-aged, unexpectedly jolly in poverty, not retarded, not the half-wit they said she was, but accepted), that there was something more than could behaviourally have been expected in the pattern. That the dye had spread out in ways only Tossie could have predicted. Who was petted on loving.

Who the people were does not matter, she thought. They are a tangle. They took their bundle of hope and put it on flat clay land, made doctors, engineers and consumptives, rag and bone men, oilmen, Indians, ferrymen. They made these streets I walk, they made the laws, they made the sallow shadow of righteousness I walk in. They thought second-hand thoughts and bore second-hand burdens. Tossie was petted on Kate, young Jamie died. Byron was bad, we always knew it. Mother got us up to 1943 and ran away. There used to be moonlight cruises down the river to Stag Island. All the rivers have Stag Islands, with little Fawns behind them. There ought to be a way of telling it.

TENTS FOR THE
GANDY-DANCERS

MR and Mrs Hector MacGregor celebrated their fiftieth wedding anniversary with roast beef, frozen fried potato puffs and champagne at the Wagon Wheel Motor Inn, a change, as Mr MacGregor remarked, from the days when only doctors could afford roast beef, champagne, divorces and liquor licenses. They watched with their usual acuity their offspring surrounding them and would have looked regal were it not for the fact that their shoulders were stooped and their faces humbled from the lengthy effort of pushing that quartet into the middle class where it had once seemed reluctant to take its rightful place. Angus, however, had been a Q.C. for several years, by this time, and was safely portly. Allistair, though still a bachelor had achieved temporary apotheosis of a sort by becoming, a year previously, temporary newsreader for the eleven o'clock news on television (thus absorbing in Mrs MacGregor's eyes some of the functions of the prime minister and some of the Deity, whose name she never used). Isobel's boy had been nominated to the Olympic Equestrian team, and Rowena, the youngest, the favorite, the easy one, had paid them the signal attention of leaving her four children at home three hundred miles away with a housekeeper. If anyone had said to them that Angus for reasons directly connected with his upbringing was now sending funds to the IRA, that Allistair was a fairy and Isobel was a lush, they would have settled back with vague smiles and said, times have changed, haven't they? They had come through two world wars, a depression, cohabitation, inflation, and a great deal else besides; their friends were dropping off from heart attacks and softening of the brain. They had done the best they could with what they had, sent three to university and one to RADA all the way over in England, and Angus to St Andrews that year he was delinquent besides, and this on Hector's commissions as a car salesman when cars were notoriously hard to sell. They had earned retirement and wasn't it grand of the children to give them a colour TV? If they were to be spared a few years alone together, they would do so, thank you, without worrying about the children; though they sometimes worried about Isobel: it was a family habit, worrying about Isobel, she wouldn't feel comfortable without it.

Rowena also worried sometimes about Isobel. Early in the spring she found her standing in the weak afternoon sun, in patched jeans and a faded plaid shirt, standing on the kitchen stool looking over the cemetery wall with a glass half-hidden in the bare ivy beside her. "Really, Isobel!"

"Hi, Rowena. How's things?"

"Fine. I was just passing and popped in to see you."

"Did Phil phone? He's been phoning again, lately."

"Heavens, no. Do you think you could lend me a spare bridge-table cover?"

"Sure, if I can remember where they are. Haven't used them since we gave all that social-schmocial stuff up." She leapt down from the stool with her glass in her hand and without spilling it. She was forty-two and meaty and her voice was deep. She hooked an arm under the stool and began to walk towards the house with Rowena.

"What were you watching?"

"Funeral. Greek, I think. Some guy in a tall hat, chanting. Looked like a wizard in a goddam fairy tale."

"You watch too many funerals."

"Yeah. Morbid, isn't it?" I kinda like the tents they put up. Some are green, some are that terra cotta sort of red, you know, flower-pot; some are yellow — not very many. Cheerful and mediaeval, if you feel that way. Hard to decide if it's convocation at McGill or the Tournament at Bosworth field or whatever it was. When there's a real posh funeral, they put green tarps on the piles of muck they've dug up and it looks like a giant's lying there with his knees up. How're the kids?"

"Fine. How's Phil?"

"Oh, you know, the usual: Phil. He doesn't like me and I don't like him. He's done the house over again since you were here at Christmas. Can't keep his hands off it."

Rowena envied Isobel the house, a big green frame one on a quadruple lot behind the cemetery. Five bedrooms and an attic, half an acre of back yard and a panelled den. Isobel never knew when she was well off. All that beautiful Knoll Associates furniture without a finger-mark on it.

When they went in, she noticed that the kitchen was now all in butcher-block wood: not a mark on that, either, probably because Isobel didn't cook any more. And the living room — there, the Knoll furniture was gone — to the office, Isobel said — and replaced by fat chunky stuff in soft unstained leather. Rowena sank down gingerly and wept inside for her worn-out chesterfield, while Isobel rummaged in cupboards. "Trouble is," said Isobel, "it doesn't look as anybody lives here, does it? Damn right it doesn't, because nobody does live here. Will one of these things do? What've the kids got now? Mumps? Chicken pox? Measles? When're you going back to work? That's what I should have done, gone back to work. Now I can't do anything but sit and drink and irritate Phil, I'm good at that all right. But never mind. In a week it's going to be time to divide the peonies. I'll get my hands back in the ground where they come from and everything will be all right again." For although Isobel disdained organisations — Phil was always urging her to join the Junior League or the University Women's Club or the Garden Club, but she maintained that anyone with only a pass B.A. in sociology style 1951 was only fit for flowers — she gardened and was famous for her foxgloves and peonies and bleeding heart and Japanese lanterns, honesty, impatience, big rich scarlet opium-looking poppies, little knob-headed zinnias, delphiniums, hollyhocks, snapdragons, asters and Albertine roses; the garden in summer was a mess of cabbages and colour and texture and kingcups. "I'm sorry you haven't got time for a drink with me. I was thinking about you just the other day.

The time Al and I took you to Tarzanland with us — did you want to come or were we supposed to be looking after you? — and you weren't as fast as we were getting through the dump on the shortcut home, and you burned a hole clear through your rubber boot and you had to go to the hospital and have a graft, poor kid. We led you a rotten chase, didn't we? Kids don't have that kind of fun any more, least not in the city."

Automatically, Rowena crossed her legs on the old scar at the memory, and drew back. She remembered. Always the one trailing behind the others. Then she smiled. "Michael says I'm tough as nails."

"We toughened you up, we did that, you poor kid. Still no harm done in the long run. I bet you keep an eye on that crew of yours."

"Davey went across Bayview last week."

"That's the beginning. God, when Robin was small I didn't know where to begin bringing up a kid in the city. We were lucky, having a whole little town to range around in. You can keep those tablecloths, I've no use for them now, but take care of the cross stitched one, it was a wedding present from Aunt Em and Uncle Frank and I still care quite a lot about them. And don't look so damn worried about me: I know who I am and where I'm going. One of these days Phil's going to have me locked up but not because there's anything wrong with *me*. We are what we are, kid, and stay out of burning dumps."

A month later, Angus ran into Isobel, who had forgotten to clean the garden out of her fingernails, at Maidie Griswold's in Rosedale. He was uncomfortable. The minute he saw her, he looked at his third wife and knew that Isobel would one day remark that like his second wife she was the spit and image of his first wife only ten years younger: and he had not thought that before he laid eyes on Isobel. Isobel was always acute. He consoled himself by looking at Phil's anxious, pinched and narrow, frightened face, and thought, God isn't Izzy the image of Marie Dressler now.

They were separated by a yard of mahogany table and a bouquet of flowers and the little girl next to him was cooing into his conch-like ear, but all he could hear was Isobel's bass voice. "You know," she was saying to a fair, polite pin-striped man beside her, "I always say to Maidie that what she's running here is a new Family Compact made out of the run-off of the old Family Compact, but the truth of it is, though I don't know you, or your wife, if she is your wife, or who you are, the rest of us are all jumped-up. Phil, now, his father was a Barnardo's boy, he's a master printer in Hamilton, still working at over 75, Phil doesn't like this story but I think it's goddam wonderful: he came over here as an orphan with his fare as a dowry and got his papers and married a housewife and bought that little stone Gothic cottage on Pearl street Phil's itching to get his hands on, and raised his one chick and gentleman, boarding school and all. Phil's had a time getting over it, of course, it's damn hard to be made the cynosure of a generation, but you can't say Creative People's not a success, Phil's agency. When I first knew him at university he wasn't a shadow of his present self — a skinny, shy, self-conscious guy, a nail-biter, but he knew what he wanted to do and he got over his background. For a while he used to say at parties, isn't it funny, my father was brought up by Syrie Maugham's daddy, and she was the very first white-paint interior decorator, and look at him now: has ten per cent of half the artistic population in the country: who else would have thought of throwing painters and decorators and copywriters and actors together?

"He used to think I was somebody because my family had been here a long time, but I disabused him of that notion, I disabused him. We were all North Irish, the lot of us, though the MacGregors thought they were better than the Lennoxes and took it out of my mother — we had terrible Christmases in Windsor with my grandma MacGregor — black Irish to the core, maiden name McAlpine — looking down on my mother, and my father was so hooked on Scottishness that the only new books we got were on clans and the only new clothes were kilts, that my mother later unpicked and turned into curtains only the light came through when she goofed with the razor blade. And we used to say we were Irish on the street to break Pa's heart. My God you should have been there the Christmas Angus hit Grandma MacGregor with a spitball when she said 'Of all the people

Hector could have married . . .' of course, all he had was Scotch-
ness and us, and we were awful kids."

Angus loosened his collar with a finger, remembering why
he had been banished to St Andrew's College, and took a bead on
his sister. She had led him over the roof in running shoes when he
had lost his and had to climb in slippery new leather boots, and
she sat by the chimney, an up-side-down red-haired Y on the
ridgepole shouting "Angus is a sucky, Angus is a sucky," eight to
his thirteen. She had got him to ride Uncle Harcourt Lennox's big
purebred sow Nell, (his legs bowed at the thought of it, the shifty
body of the beast careening under him, his knees gripped the slippery filthy hairy sides, his arms fled upwards and his ear tore
again against the old eavestrough, rusty, and bled like a . . . he
looked at Phil, superb in his aristocratic distance. My god she had
met her match in Phil.

"Maidie," Isobel said, "Now Maidie . . ."

"Now Isobel," said Maidie, "we're leaving the gentlemen."

"It's pretentious, but I'll go if I have to," said Isobel. Nobody
laughed.

On the way home Angus's wife said, "Your sister sat and
stared at me all the time she was talking."

"What was she talking about?"

"Interior decorators."

"With Maidie?"

"No, a little woman in a beige silk dress. I bet it cost a
couple of hundred dollars and was supposed to look shabby."

"Linda Mayfield."

"She started it. She was talking about having her house done
over. Why does Phil do theirs every year?"

"Habit. Cover up the drink-rings. Who knows. He started as
a decorator."

"Oh, I know that, I heard all about it, at length. And then
she said, of course at home you never had decorators, you just left
things where they were. She was joking about getting your room
when you were sent to boarding school. You never told me you
went to boarding school."

"Only for a year."

"Anyhow, she said she got your room when you left and

there was a framed, illuminated copy of a poem called "IF" over the bed, and she believed every word of it."

"She would."

"She said that even if you never had your house decorated, every few years a man came and painted the doors cream and then painted them brown, and then ran a kind of comb through the brown when it was still wet to make a wood-grain pattern."

"I'd forgotton that."

"I saw a cute little table like that downtown yesterday. It would go in the front hall. It's only a hundred dollars, Angus."

Angus shuddered.

Allistair was drying his wig with the blower when the phone rang. He told Shimon "If it's Isobel, tell her I'm out."

"No, it's Phil."

He turned the blower off and twirled the wig on his hand as he talked. "Hi, Phil."

"Hi, Al. I just thought I'd phone and tell you — somebody, anybody — I've just taken Isobel to the Institute."

"My God, what happened?"

"Nothing, that I remember. She was drunker than usual last night and she tried to slit her wrists."

"Poor you."

"Poor Izzy."

"Don't be a hypocrite, Phil."

"At any rate, they're going to dry her out and see what they can do for her."

"Visitors?"

"I'll let you know."

Later in the week he ran into Isobel's doctor at a party. "How's my sister?"

"Frankly, I don't know. Not yet. Have you been to see her?"

"Phil said no visitors yet."

"I'd have let you in, if I'd known. She likes you."

"I know that, to my rue."

"Lunch next week?"

"Sure." These were hungry days for Allistair.

"I'll meet you at the Israeli place Tuesday at one."

"She tells wonderful stories," said Morgan H. Frye, "wonderful stories. What I wanted to know from you, is, are they true? Professionally speaking, of course, it doesn't matter: the story arises from the need to tell the story, the content is illustrative of the need, the fabric is single. But privately, I keep wondering, is it all true? Did you go to a farm in the summer?"

"Sure, we went to three or four of them. My mother had all these lovely brothers in overalls with crates of new-laid eggs under their arms. Rows and rows of hired men tilting their chairs back against the kitchen wall, tickling us. Hayseed in the hair, rime on the spray, wonderful."

"Did you really let the cows lick your knees?"

"I found it a little sick-making myself. Can you imagine anyone licking Izzy's knees?"

"And the hired men put mangles through the mangle and there were snake fences and hawthorn trees?"

"Uh-huh, and bees in a glen sort of place, and the ghost of Mickey Doolin across the road where his house had fallen in.

"Who was he?"

"Did she leave that one out? It's one of the good ones. He died on his farm, and his sister was up from Philadelphia to keep him company, and she drank and she came over the road screaming like a banshee he was dead, get the undertaker, get the undertaker; only of course there wasn't any undertaker, so my mother and her youngest brother, the one who died at Passchendaele went over. The women were scared to touch him, but Bob, who was about nine, went about the business of dressing him in his best suit, closing his eyes with pennies, and all; and then when he was straightening his pants out, his foot twitched good and proper, and he and my mother both wet their pants and the sister from Philadelphia had an epileptic fit, and for fifty years after kids ran like hell when they had to pass his house at night."

"Did a lot of women up there die in childbirth?"

"I think there were grisly stories Mother used to tell the girls: a horrid one about blood coming through the ceiling."

"And whenever there was a new baby . . ."

"Gramma Lennox was up that hill with her brolly under her arm in a minute."

"What's Philip like?"

"You've met him."

"You know him. Apparently you get on with him."

"Well don't label him just because of little old me, dear. He isn't bent. I'm very fond of Phil, and I don't know what I'd have done without him after I quit the CBC. Of course just because I like him, Isobel doesn't have to. She hates him."

"Why?"

"Oh, I don't know. You know Izzy, she's contrary, always has been. There was something about another man years ago and he took her back and forgave her when she really wanted him to toss her out; and then of course there was the row about sending Robin to boarding school. She was furious about that."

"Why? Possessiveness?"

"No, I don't think so, not really, I saw her through that one, she was in a dog's rage for months, foaming at the mouth. It wouldn't have been so bad if they'd chosen one of the progressive ones, but sending him off to become a little gentleman at that grey stone place — she saw it as a violation of every democratic ideal that had been banged into us at home: I mean if we stood for anything at home, we stood for neighbourhoods, egalitarianism, that sort of thing. Of course Robin was glad enough to go; they used to fight something dreadful over him."

"What's he like, now?"

"Beautiful. Red hair. He rides. She should have worked, Isobel."

"She says the only job she ever had was out west in the summer cooking for the gandy-dancers."

"Does she, now, and who are they?"

"The men who repair the railways and go up and down the tracks in gangs on jiggers."

"Oh, those push-me pull-you things. No, she never went west, unless it was with Phil for a holiday. The first summer that she was at university she worked up at Elgin House with me — I was a bus boy, she was a waitress. After that she used to go home and work in the library, she liked being on the lake. It was some cousin of ours from the farm, there was one farm where it never rained, it was under a hill or something, and they couldn't make

154

ends meet, and he went west to the harvest, and she cooked for the gandy-dancers. They were called Almer and Phyllis, something rural like that. Will she get better, our Iz?"

"There's nothing essentially wrong with her except the drink."

"She's a bitch, Isobel. It's a game she plays with Phil. She should have gone to sea. She was always trying to get me to go to sea because she couldn't. Years later, she found out women could get into the Norwegian navy, and ever since she's been taking it out on Phil."

"Why?"

"Ask her. I never married, I wouldn't know."

Angus was doing the Kingsley Double-Crostic in his office to avoid looking at his bank statement when his secretary showed in a large policeman; who asked if he knew a woman named Flossie Mackenzie. "I can't say I do," he said.

Well, she had jumped off a subway platform in front of the train at Rosedale with his name on a bit of paper in her pocket, could he come to Lombard street and identify her?

He knew before he got there who she was. He took a look at her and phoned Phil. They went around to the room she had rented on Sherbourne street after she left the hospital, to pay the landlord and collect her things. A few old clothes in the suitcase she had used to take to and from the university, a carton of cigarettes, some books — mostly Collins red leather classics from home — an ashtray she had made herself in occupational therapy, a stack of exercise books. Angus offered these to Phil, who shook his head. "I'll give them to Allistair," he said.

The funeral was heavily attended by clients of Phil's agency. Allistair, cadaveral in black, read the 23rd Psalm as she had asked in her will. Her parents had not come, they were unwell and unable to travel. Rowena wept. She was not buried in her neighbourhood cemetery.

Angus went back to his office afterwards and flipped through the pile of notebooks he had not, after all, given Allistair. Indecipherable scribbles, meaningless jottings. Pages divided crookedly in half with ballpoint lines: "Cavaliers" "Roundheads"

"Introverts," "Extroverts", "Male, Female" — nothing under these headings he could make out. Handwriting slanting every which way. "Come, little leaves, said the wind one day," he deciphered. That was from the old first-grade reader. Then, heavily underlined, "You'll be a man, my son." Crazy stuff. He threw the notebooks in the wastebasket and went back to the crossword puzzle, wondering what he was going to do about that damnfool Diarmuid Ryan and the bazookas.

Phil let Allistair live in the house while he and Robin were away in Europe in the summer. He was sitting in the exquisite Japanese Garden when Robin came home. Phil had gone straight on to see a client in New York.

"How was your trip?"

"Fine. Sure, fine." Robin was twenty, now, a picture of sophistication and fine tailoring, with just an endearing corner of gawkiness left.

"How's Phil?"

"Oh, he's okay now. He moped a lot at first, but he's okay now. You know, for a while in Paris he sat in the seats reserved for the *mutiles de guerre* in the metro and felt sorry for himself, but he's okay now."

Allistair looked at Robin and knew that he was now expected to find another place to live. He made a great, sweeping gesture with his hand. "I think I liked the garden better the way it was before," he said spitefully.

RUTH

SHE had a red dress that had been a cousin's and was old and soft. The hem pulled off in the hedges when she was playing cowboys. Her mother was mad; but she remembered the soft ripping noise and making it into a bandage.

She had jacks and a little rubber ball. The Grade One teacher caught her shifting the ball from cheek to cheek and said she was a dirty little thing, a disgrace, and kept her in. It was hard to explain at the end of the day, so she cried and wet her pants and that distracted them.

She was playing on the front steps with her ball and her jacks, getting nowhere, and the radio that was shaped like a church window was on the verandah; her father had just finished rewiring the aerial because it rained last night so they took it in. The King came on the radio to say the war was on. He sounded sad, and she already knew he stuttered because he was left handed and had been changed, which was why they hadn't changed her. She was counting loud at her jacks and her father shushed her. "Yah old piss," she yelled at him, and ran away. He paid no attention, which hurt most of all.

Her mother was big; wore grey; rode a bicycle; wore shoes with cuban heels. When the Americans started to make a fuss about Cuba, she knew what they meant.

The library was the only safe place. Otherwise you had to tramp the street beside those heels, and the grey hems. Down in the basement of the library there was a stuffed alligator and a globe of the world; an ingle-nook by a fireplace with yellow glass coal in it; a lot of books with faded, complicated pictures in them; the trees had knuckles.

Her father went away and died in the war, as she had known he would. She went to church with her brother and Mrs Watson. Her mother sang in the choir, sang solos, and when her mother sang she wanted to die of humiliation. She buried her face in Mrs Watson's cuffs, on Mrs Watson's winter coat of many colours. She never found out who Mrs Watson was.

The church was white brick turned grey, with Gothic-shaped windows and a square tower, and a Sunday school hall with cast-iron seats and railings. In the church were 63 organ pipes, painted gold, like pencils with a piece scraped out of the front, as if you were sharpening them too high up and hit the lead. The choir sat below the organ pipes in black gowns and mortar boards, like university graduates, which her mother was and the others weren't. After the war they got soft maroon mortarboards and maroon gowns with gold satin dickies; so they looked like Transylvanian university graduates with wattles. She was not religious, reality kept intruding; the church was a big thing in their lives. She herself helped her mother run the Communion grapejuice through the jelly bag, and went over Sunday nights to help Mrs Northcott wash Communion cups and dry them on the end of her little finger, with a linen teatowel. One of the elders held up her mother's Gem jar and said one night, "Well, girls, wanna finish it up?" It had been explained to her that the blood of Christ was a metaphor, but still in church she thought of squeezing the puce-coloured jelly bag between her hands, never managing to get it tight the way her mother did — she had aggressive elbows — the feel of the blood of Christ oozing out of the puce-coloured linsey-woolsey or whatever it was: she was not religious. The body of Christ came from Christie's bread.

They said she ought to be able to rise above the feeling and she cried in front of her whole (mixed) Sunday school class.

After the war the church decorators came through and painted the Baptist church yellow, Sacred Heart blue, St Andrew's pink and their church, the big rich one, a mixture of all colours, rose, green, fawn, peach; with borders of stencilled gold fleurs-delis.

Her mother became head of the classics department in the Collegiate. This created a climate of respect and no one but the English teacher asked Ruth any questions. That suited her.

Because eventually her mother stopped trying to teach her to play the piano, clapping loud in her ear ONE two three, ONE two three, saving money on the metronome; and got busy, very busy; and even went sometimes to the movies with Mr Galloway, until someone pointed out that even if Mrs Galloway was a chronic invalid this was not proper; so then they went on separate nights and Mr Galloway came on a third night and they sat in rocking chairs on the porch very far from each other and talked about their movies. Ruth's mother wanted her to come with her but the fact was with movies and choir practice and Mr Galloway at least in summer she had three nights a week of beautiful silence inside the house. And she didn't care for Anne Todd, Phyllis Calvert, or Margaret Lockwood.

Other nights she went to Young Peoples' or The Canadian Girls in Training. She was not a Girl Guide. She had been a Brownie over at the Anglican church but she was too diffident to push her way in the line to do the knot-tests, and failed them all.

In winter, when she was little, she was always late home from school, because if you went the long complicated way you could pass the foundry, and the men would open the big sliding doors and you could stand with the other kids in a careful half circle watching men naked to the waist pulling long-handled shovels out of the great furnaces; and as the molten metal hit the air sparks flew up and the children all cried "AAAAh," and the men's sweat gleamed. But if you lingered too long, the boys chased you with frozen horsebuns, the warm spark went out of the air, it was cold, the long thumbs of your mittens were sodden and frozen, you wet your wool snowpants, it froze, they chafed your thighs between the tops of your stockings and your combed navy-blue overpants, you smelled when you got home, you snivelled because she was mad, there were burrs in your hair from crossing the railway cut . . . misery and glory went together.

The people were said to be warm and friendly but they watched you. They always knew where you were going, if you didn't know.

And she always knew where they were going. Because she watched them.

She watched them and tried to peel them like grapes and get the skin off them, but she never quite could. They were always capable of being unexpected but never capable enough. She thought she was the only one who read the books in the library, but one night the elder came to give out communion cards and pray with her mother who was at the movies; and instead of praying with Ruth he picked up *A Room of One's Own* and spoke eloquently of how *A Writer's Diary* meant more to him than any book except the Bible. A man with a grey face who wore sleeve garters and sock garters and sold insurance. She could not believe him. Any more than, at that time, she understood *A Room of One's Own* except the need.

"I love you," she said to Boris, when she was just past seventeen.

"Kid," said Boris, running his beautiful hands over her once again, "eat something you can't eat, like cardboard. It will go away."

Boris was beautiful and worked in the library. He had chamber music records and paintings, some he had done himself, which were good; because he was not an amateur; he had given up painting and become a librarian. Her mother was on the library board. That summer she owned a blue dress, New Look, with buttons every two inches, and he had opened each one and kissed them. Just once. She was running a day camp for underprivileged children, at the time.

"Boris," her mother said, "is too intellectual."

"He likes Handel, Mum."

"His taste is too intellectual. He won't buy any new mysteries. He won't buy Grace Livingston Hill. He doesn't like Gene Stratton Porter. He's filling the library up with Henry Green. He wants to buy Henry Miller, who is banned. His taste is sordid."

"He gave me Charles Williams to read. I like him."

She sniffed. "High Anglican. Though I don't object to him. Still, Boris ought to be careful. The reality of life is, that if members of the Board can't get what they want to read, they will fire the librarian." She told Boris to be careful and he took her two hands and looked her deep, deep, deep in the eyes and said he was, and then laughed. And never touched her again. When she was forty she wondered if all the rest of her life was not a sort of Boris deprivation, and then dismissed the idea. Boris was old now, and he drank.

As all persons of good family are advised to do, she went to university. At the one she went to, everyone — no, that was untrue — some of the people were very religious. She had not the knack of being asked out (she was small and vague-looking, she was not good at clothes, she read, but never laughed) so she was home every night in Residence. Two women in Leadership Training took to coming to her room each night to pray, as her roommate was always out. She had thought she had come to university to read and said so, and ran into an argument that ran back to grape-juice and the Blood of Christ. She fell behind in her work, she fell into despair, she wanted to kill them but still somehow knelt beside them beside her army-issue bottom bunk, with her forehead on a grey army blanket, praying for them to go away. She did not want to be a better girl than she was.

Her prayers were not answered. She did not manage to get them to go away. She went home for Easter and told her mother she was leaving the university. Her mother was galvanised and went so far as to drive down to see the Dean of Women, who was also religious. She could not tell her about the two women, one of whom had the face of a moon-calf, an Egyptian god; one of whom was fat, with flesh of white clay; who knelt beside her praying for her. Every night that Lyall was out. They sat headlocked together and Ruth repeated that she did not wish to stay. She had no friends. No one had asked her out. There were no parties and dances. The French club did not interest her, or Fencing and Archery. Anyway it was agony, too late. She went home and got a job in the Hydro office.

When she was forty she woke with a searing pain. Only it was not a pain. It was, she recognised, a searing cry of sexual distress. Beside her, her husband slumbered. She got out of bed and pulled open the curtains and dressed. Standing first naked by the window, for the lake was blue and the air had the first softness of spring. She wanted clothes of that air, and she wanted —who, what — how? What she wanted was sex, and she could taste it.

Though it was tangled up with other things: the first books read, initial impulses, water, green leaves, reactions. She wanted Boris enough to sit down like a wolf and howl for him. She did not want her husband. Maybe her son or her daughter, but not her husband. Nothing old, nothing blue: air, sea, light, green leaves, remembrance.

She carried the feeling around with her like a nail. She had gone through a promiscuous stage and bought the first bikini ever seen there and taken on God knows whom and paid for it. Now it was back again, pepper in the nose, and she was six and sixteen and twenty.

She was rich, now. After saving her money at the Hydro she had bought lake property because she could. It was twenty-five dollars a foot, then. Now it was twenty times that. She had money, she was married, beside her a good man snoozed. And the spring sun brought a good-awful stab of lust, an electric pencil in the innards. Time. Remembrance.

Boris was old, now. And she had declined to join the post-marital ritual dance on the beach. She was superior, always superior. She let no corporation executives, no oil engineers, into her house. Now when the sweet stab swept over her, darting like the Holy Ghost, all she could do was go down to the shore and stroke the sand flanks of her land.

She looked at her husband while he slept. He was beautiful in repose. He looked tanned, carved, like a statue. If he knew, she thought, if he knew. That I squeezed the blood of Christ out of the jelly bag, crinch, crinch, crinch, but my hands were never as strong as Mother's were.

BICYCLE STORY

D O you remember what it was like to be a child? Do you remember as you stand there with the wooden spoon in your hand threatening, do you remember? A child. A victim. Not the happy skippy thing you see on the street there, but a real child, the kind you were? Harrowed. Interrupted. Sullied. Spilled.

They were so big and always after you and they never left you alone. I remember now. Since yesterday I have remembered.

I was driving down Cobden Street at two o'clock in the afternoon. The daffodils were pushing out of their sheathes, the birds were making a racket in the sky, and I was thinking, was it Cobden's *Rural Rides* I always meant to read or Cobbett's? That is what I have thought on Cobden Street for at least twenty years; and Marshallene came on the CBC to talk about a new novel she had written about us all. "Childhood is not what you think it is," she was saying, and things fell together for me, the way they perhaps did for Saul on the way to Damascus, Proust on a Paris curb. And my mother came shooting out of an alleyway on her bicycle, and I ran over her.

My mother is six feet tall and seventy-two years old. She has been riding that bicycle ever since I can remember, but particularly since my father went away to the war in 1940 and put the Rockney up on blocks in the garage. I could tell you more about my father, or about the car, which my brother sold years later as an antique, but it isn't necessary.

BICYCLE STORY

My mother's favorite poem is "Old Meg, She was a Gypsy," but she is too practical ever to have lived upon the moors or slept on the brown heath turf. When she heard that my father had died in 1941, she got her old job back teaching Latin at the Collegiate. She was a good teacher. She had perhaps no deep notion of the poetry of that language, but in the school system in Ontario, then, Latin was used as a substitute for instructing us in pagan Greek logic; it was a guide to dispassionate, methodical thinking, a method of ordering one's thoughts. She was good at conveying this, she had and still has a great talent for order, for separating, sorting and categorising things in useful ways. When you did Caesar with her the world was an orderly, pleasant place where the boats were neatly drawn up on the shore (Cycle One). There were other Latin teachers at our school, whose classes I sat in until Upper School.

It was in that last year I understood how good she was.

But before that last year, when I was very little, before my father died, she taught music lessons. She had no metronome. She clapped her big firm palms together by her pupils' ears to make them get the rhythm right. *"One,* two, three, *one,* two, three, it's a waltz, get it right, Ruth Ann, get it right."

She was very big and I was very little, a definitely weaker vessel, a foolish virgin. My brother was four years older, and lived a mysterious life involving Big-Little books and tree houses. I, who complain even when the gentlest flutes rise in chamber music, trembled at the volume of robin-song and fainted beside my mother on the piano bench. Never learned to ride a bicycle, never made friends with any of the dogs, the big half-Indian collies (the kind with brown underhair and coal-black backs, brown eyebrows: Indian dogs) who panted after her on her bicycle. I lived a secret life in the quietest corner of the children's library, poring over books with treasure-maps and faint Victorian illustrations, there in the inglenook between the globe and brown leering stuffed alligator. A brown-eyed lady the size of an elf brought me book after book and lured me to my mother when the day was over, saying, "But she's no trouble at all, Mrs Macrae."

I understand that my father was also small.

I grew up and left her house. She lives there still, though as times and salaries improved she changed it: took the harsh brown fuzz off the chesterfield that scraped your bare legs, and had the sink and pump in the pantry changed to a shining stainless-steel basin with taps. For a while she rented rooms to young men in industry. Now she's alone by preference, she's "getting on" she doesn't want to have anyone to do for. Her house is softer and quieter now, with rugs instead of linoleum, and pink and yellow walls and curtains instead of the oranges and maroons and violent greens of my childhood. It's less harrowing. Though I don't see much of her, since she's convinced I spoil my children.

I was driving quietly down Cobden Street listening to Marshallene on the radio, and she was talking about childhood, and Mother, still wearing her black watch winter slacks and her bicycle clips and her dark green nylon ski jacket, shot out of the alley with Lucky panting behind her, and I braked, but not soon enough, and knocked her down.

I got out of the car and ran to her, and so did Mr Walker the postman, and Mrs Ferns came out on her porch and started to scream. Mother said, "Nonsense, Emily," to Mrs Ferns, and "My goodness, Ruthann, you always were absent minded," to me. With tears in my eyes I reached down to help her up, and Lucky bit me, tore a vein in the back of my hand. It was for me they called the ambulance.

"Marshallene was on the radio," I said weakly, and, "Mother, call off your damned dog," and a lot of other things, I suppose, leaning against the front fender of my car, not worrying about the traffic piling up behind. I'm not very good about blood. Mother adjusted her lumber jacket and brushed the dirt off her trousers and tried to pick up her bicycle. Then she found her collarbone was broken, so we went to the hospital together.

"She's a character, your mother," the policeman said.

"She's marvellous," I said, as brightly as I could because his tourniquet was pinching.

"Then it's her dog you were after, was it?" he asked. "After all, there's such a thing as a Freudian slip."

"Whatever are you thinking about?" I heard myself ask in her own voice and gestures. "She rides like a bat out of hell, you know."

165

"You ought to have thought of that and been careful in her neighbourhood."

"We live, I mean, she lives, 'way over on Batten street." Oh, I might have told him I was listening to Marshallene on the radio, but what can you tell a cop? Though he sounded a good deal more interesting than most of the ones I've met in this town. We're getting our cops as well as our ministers from Belfast now, it seems. So I asked him how I could get in touch with my husband, the lawyer, and he spoke into his radio. And then the ambulance came and I lay down and passed out. I don't know who parked the car.

By the time I got to the hospital my hand was swollen badly, and I was glad to see Barney, about whom my mother said the day before I married him, that at least he'd never let me down (as if one day I'd regret this, as I have, and how did she know?) When the x-rays were done it was clear I was worse off than Mother who was holding court in Emergency asking the out-patients what church they went to and explaining how they could help by patronising the Women's Auxiliary booth in the hospital lobby, and wondering if bursitis would set in, and striking her knee, and laughing, and saying it was funny, poor absent-minded Ruthie listening to Marshallene and running her own mother down. Barney got Doctor Parkison in, who knew what shots would go with her digitalis. She didn't want to stay all night in the hospital but we talked her into it.

I tried to explain it all to Barney, but he looked impatient and shook his head and said he wished I liked my mother better. "But I *do* like her," I said.

"Has she laid a charge?"

"Not so to speak."

"You'll lose points off your license."

"I don't care if I ever drive again except that Sheila will have to quit ballet. You know I didn't do it on purpose, don't you?"

"Who thinks you did?"

"The Irish policeman. Mother, perhaps."

"That's the trouble with places this size, isn't it? Whoever you knock down is bound to be a relation. Still, you hit the jackpot. What are you going to do now? Who's at home?

"Shirley should be there by now. I'm worried about picking

up Sheila."

"I one-upped you there. Phoned the school and told her to skip her lesson and take the bus home. Want to come out for a drink with me now you're more or less finished here?"

"I think I'd better stay and see what's happening with Mother. She's very excited. I don't like it." Not that I was going to look after her, but it seemed only decent to keep her company.

By the time my hand was stitched up, her shoulder was taped, her arm was in a sling, and she was sitting in bed looking gaunter than I had seen her look before, and inappropriate under a crucifix as well.

"I don't know how to say I'm sorry," I said to her.

Her grey hair was spread untidily against the pillows. She was never neat. And the shot that had calmed her took away the animation that made her look young.

"It must have been a shock to you, Ruthie."

"You don't mind staying here for a night? Dr. Parkinson says it's been a shock to you as well. You'll sleep a bit here. If you go home you'll be roaming around the house and making cups of tea all night."

"I'd just like Barney to go over and put food out for Lucky. I told him to go home, I don't know whether he will or not."

"Barney said he'd look after that. And he's going to get your bicycle fixed as well."

"Barney's a reliable man. Sometimes I don't know how you had the sense to marry him."

I look at my hands in my lap, not daring to say the things she said about Barney, once, how his parents drank, how they were worldly people who would lead me into bad ways. Before she knew him well, of course.

"What was Marshallene saying on the CBC? She's been on a lot, lately, hasn't she?"

"Rather pleasant things. About how there were details about this country that had never been written down. And then something that made me remember almost too much: how it wasn't easy to be a child."

She sniffed. "How it isn't easy to be a mother, if she knew the whole of it. You never knew, did you, how things were in their house, why she was sent to us?"

"A little of it. Only a little. Funny, today I remembered the day she came, remember? Mrs Heber turning up at the door with Marshallene and those two little red-headed twins, Johnnie and Joan . . . "

"Joanne," she corrected, "Millie liked fancy names."

"Anyway Marshallene marched in as if she owned the place, but the twins were nice and shy. You told me to get down a sealer of grandma's orange drink and as I was doing it I prayed and prayed you'd take the twins and not Marshallene."

"How did you know I was going to take anyone at all?"

"I don't know. There were emotions flying around. There was something final and — portentous I guess — about the way they came in."

"Oh, he was a bad lot, that Walter. And Byron in trouble with the law all the time, and the two boys lost overseas. Millie was just a slip of a thing when she married him, and an American. She didn't know anything about what he was like. He'd been that way since childhood, a regular charmer when he got his own way, but holy jumped-up Judas, as your father used to say, when he lost his temper he was a fierce, black man. She met him at one of those dances they used to have when there were summer boats on the river — my they were pretty affairs, though I never ran with that crowd. All he gave her was a baby every year — they used to call him Walter the Mick, it wasn't nice, was it? but people are tough. I'd never thought I'd encourage a woman to leave her husband, but when I saw her that day — he'd broken her false teeth in a fit of rage, I just said come on in Millie.

"She wanted to get Marshallene some kind of job as a maid, but she was only twelve and anyway you know what happens to highschool girls in that sort of situation.

"You never liked Marshallene, did you? You felt she put you in the shade. You were jealous of her."

"She was big and dark and strong like you. I felt over-powered. And she did anything she wanted, and put the blame on me."

"She'd grown up the hard way, Ruthie. It wouldn't have been Christian to let her go out for a maid. And it was good for you to have another girl around."

"Yes, I guess so." Grudgingly, still.

She climbed out the window and, wearing Mother's best evening gown from the 'thirties from the trunk in the basement, sang the "Bells of St Mary's" at Talent Nite at the Imperial Theatre. She'd stop in at Patsy Rembauer's on the way to school and change her decent white shirt for a see-through nylon blouse even if she had to change back in the locker room during fourth period when Mother caught up with her. She was so strong she convinced all of us we were fat, when she was and we never dared say it to her. And every night her bobby-pins fell plink-plink-plink in a plug-tobacco tin as she curled her hair. She came from the country and knew about things we didn't, and she walked out of the VD film they showed at CGIT, and refused to go to Normal School. She broke all the rules and God never struck her down with lightning after all.

"She's done well, Marshallene," I said to my mother. "She's been a credit to you."

Mother raised herself up on her good elbow with a groan, winced, looked at me suspiciously. "Goodness, you're flattering me. You must be afraid I'd lay charges against you. I'll live the night. I'm upset at what Lucky's done to your hand. I wonder if I should have him destroyed. He's fourteen, he's old and bad-tempered like me. Still, you've never got on with dogs, have you? I wonder who you're like, you always seemed to be my changeling, small and sensitive. Gran Macrae was small, of course and so was your father. No, you felt Marshallene put you in the shade, and you've always held my taking her in against me."

"Not really, Mum. Not since I grew up and understood. I'd do the same myself."

"Things were bad, there. It didn't really get better on those farms even in the 'forties. It never has, around here. You were lucky, I was lucky. You look all in, go home and get some sleep, child."

So I took a taxi, but when I got home and saw Shirley had left the kitchen a mess and Barney had left the kids alone and gone to the Library Board meeting (though that's really all right now Sheila is 12), I couldn't settle to anything. It's hard to concentrate when your house has been left to other people since you've just knocked your mother off a bike. I wandered around the house like a silent banshee, picking up a sock here and a cookie there, wondering what to do with myself, knowing it had been an accident for me but not for other people. I thought I'd settle down with a drink and watch television but in four seconds I was bored and in five I was pleasantly high: I'd had some shots that obviously didn't go with alcohol. I picked up the phone and asked Toronto information if they had a listing for Marshallene Osborne.

"Gosh, I've been thinking of you," she said. "How are you?"

"Fine. I heard you on the radio today and I thought, it's years since I've talked to Marshallene."

"Nine years. How are the kids?"

"Growing up. How's Roby?"

"Great, just great. What was I saying on the CBC? The usual nonsense?"

"How there were a lot of things here that hadn't been written down."

"Oh, that. They come around with their microphones and I say what pops in my head and get paid for it. It's grand. You and Barney are still there and still together, eh? How's your Mum?"

"Grand. Steaming along like anything. Still riding a bicycle." I had no intention of telling her about the accident: she'd have it all over the magazines in a month.

"You know, there're a lot of things I've been meaning to ask you. Like, what happened to Al Webber?"

"He's a psychiatrist. He drinks."

"That stands to reason. Remember that summer, eh?"

"Vividly. You took him away from me."

"You didn't miss much. You know my father's dead?"

"No, I didn't hear about that."

"You don't read the county notes in the paper, eh? They got him a heart-pacer in London but eventually even that wore out and he died two months ago, the old bastard. The house is up for sale and John and I are thinking of coming up this summer and going through it, not that he had anything to leave."

"Nothing much changes up here."

"I bet your mother still barrels down the street on her bike with her dog running after her."

"She never goes out without him. Different dog, but the same, if you know what I mean."

"She's a great old character. I'll have to do a book about her some time. We'll get together this summer. I want to have a last look at the old farm, and to see your house again, and your mother. I guess I gave you a bad time, but she really made me, you know. Without her I'd have thought six kids and the prize at talent night was the apex of existence."

Her voice didn't sound far away. I felt her there, beside me in my own house. I shifted away from her a little, avoiding the big hips and the red, red lips and the big personality; the roll-up bangs and the knowing voice. I could hear her saying in another life, "All you have to do is climb out the window, stupid." And, "Not that kind of bra, stupid, the kind with strings, you stick out better. Your Ma doesn't know from nothing about brassieres. She thinks they cause cancer. Well, they don't. And mascara doesn't make you blind, either."

And Ma, from on high, in her church choir mortarboard and yellow satin jabot, was saying in my head half-bitterly, "You can say what you like about Marshallene, but she's a worker, Ruthie, she's a worker."

Marshallene went on talking about her family for a full twelve minutes, because if there were two 'lost' in the war and one in the pen, there were lots left over. Finally, I hung up on her and went to bed, and fell asleep right away.

I woke up this morning and the weather was glorious. My hand hurt, but not very badly. Barney left, the kids went to school fairly easily, I turned off the radio and on the silence and sat down with the paper and a cup of coffee. I looked around the kitchen: it wasn't tidy but it was my own.

Dr Parkinson phoned and said if I didn't mind he'd like to keep Mother in the hospital another day for tests now he had her lying still. I said he shouldn't keep her longer unless something was wrong, it would upset her to be so still. He agreed. I said I'd visit her in the afternoon.

I sat down again and the most enormous contentment settled

down on me. I couldn't quite account for it, it was foreign to me, nothing I was used to. Then I realised that I really, at last, had my life in order. The doctor was doing what I said with Mother. And at last I had power over Mother; it had taken all these years, but now she was in my grip. I could buy her a ten-speed racer or make her get rid of that Lucky (who had bitten many postmen). And that if Marshallene came, all bulk and charm and red lipstick, in the summer, I could tell lies to her or I could snub her.

No one, I thought, in my house, was ever going to drop bobby-pins one by one into an Old Plug tin, or imitate Deanna Durbin, or hang over me clapping her hands. So my hand hurt. Not very much. I opened the window and told the birds they could sing.